Praise for

⊷┤ THE LIBRARY OF EVER ├⊶

"Zeno Alexander's *The Library of Ever* reads
like someone mixed Neil Gaiman with Chris
Grabenstein, then threw in an extra dash of charm.
Reading it is like getting lost in an entire library
full of books, and never wanting to leave!"

—JAMES RILEY,
New York Times–bestselling author of
the Story Thieves series

✦

"For passionate library fans."

—*SCHOOL LIBRARY JOURNAL*

✦

"Delightful . . . A whirlwind of characters and
events in time and space . . . This book is for
every person who has ever believed that
libraries are magic."

—*BOOKLIST*

✦

"A fast-paced adventure set in a magical library
that had me smiling all the way."

—*GEEKMOM*

THE LIBRARY OF EVER

ZENO ALEXANDER

[Imprint]
MAKE YOUR MARK

NEW YORK

SQUARE
FISH

An imprint of Macmillan Publishing Group, LLC
120 Broadway, New York, NY 10271
mackids.com

Square Fish and the Square Fish logo are trademarks of Macmillan and
are used by Imprint under license from Macmillan.

Our books may be purchased in bulk for promotional, educational,
or business use. Please contact your local bookseller or the
Macmillan Corporate and Premium Sales Department at (800) 221-7945
ext. 5442 or by email at MacmillanSpecialMarkets@macmillan.com.

ISBN 978-1-250-23370-7 (paperback)   ISBN 978-1-250-16916-7 (ebook)

[Imprint]
MAKE YOUR MARK

@ImprintReads
Imprint logo designed by Amanda Spielman
Originally published in the United States by Imprint
First Square Fish edition, 2020
Book designed by Ellen Duda
Square Fish logo designed by Filomena Tuosto

1   3   5   7   9   10   8   6   4   2

LEXILE: 820L

Good friend, for Zeno's sake forbear,
To steal the words enclos'ed here.
Blessed be the ones who scorn the crooks
And cursed be they who thieve my books.

To the heroine who saved me

CONTENTS

~ THE ~
LIBRARY
OF EVER

CHAPTER ONE
Lenora Arrives

Lenora was wretchedly unhappy.

She was wretchedly unhappy despite the fact that she was lounging in the back of a giant limousine, so wretchedly unhappy that she had thrown herself across an entire leather seat and was kicking away at one of the doors. She was wretchedly unhappy despite having incredibly rich parents and an inattentive nanny, despite everything. They'd stuck her with this nanny while they were gone. Normally an inattentive nanny would be wonderful, but this nanny insisted on dragging Lenora all over the city in her parents' limo so the nanny could see her friends and shop and do every boring thing an adult could possibly want to do. Lenora had to go along for all of it, and she was BORED. BORED. BORED.

She'd tried everything to make it an interesting summer. "Look!" she'd said to her mother, who was selecting her most glamorous dresses for the trip Lenora wasn't going on. "The planetarium is hiring an assistant. I could apply!"

"Nonsense, Lenora!" her mother had said.

"But why not? I love the stars." And she did, even though she could hardly see them, living in the big, bright city her entire life. "How about this? The art museum is hiring a tour guide!"

"Ridiculous!"

"And the zoo's big cat habitat is hiring someone to feed the tigers . . ."

"Preposterous!"

"But WHY?" asked Lenora, sure that she could do any of these things if given the chance.

"Because none of those places is going to hire an eleven-year-old," stated her father, who was in the other closet trying to decide which of his five hundred ties to bring. "Now, stop being silly and do try to get along with the nanny. She comes from a very good family."

And so Lenora found herself lying flat on her back across the incredibly comfortable limousine seat and staring up through the window at passing skyscrapers. She thought about how bored she was and kicked at the door of the limo again.

"Stop that," said the nanny as she tapped away at her phone. She was sitting several feet away on her own seat.

Lenora pushed herself up enough to look out at the passing city, its museums and parks with trees for climbing and sculpture gardens all blurring by. So many wonderful things out there in the vast world, and she was exploring absolutely none of them. All this on a day when she'd worn her favorite loose, comfortable dress, hoping for some excitement. "Where are we going now?" she asked. The nanny had spent the morning rushing from one horrid boutique to another, buying herself dresses for parties while Lenora sprawled on chairs with nothing to do. Yesterday it had been perfume shops all day long. Lenora wanted to know what fresh nightmares awaited her this afternoon.

"To the library," said the nanny. "Now shush, I'm one marshmallow away from winning a gold sparrow."

Lenora perked up. "The library? You? Why?"

"I'm checking out a book to impress the friend I'm visiting later."

Lenora sat up completely. "Can I go to the children's section?" With a stack of books beside her, she thought, she wouldn't be bored for days and days.

"No," said the nanny.

We'll see about that, thought Lenora. The nanny was, after all, quite inattentive.

Their chauffeur let them out on the front steps of the library and leaned back against the limo and unfolded his newspaper.

"Don't get comfortable," the nanny warned him. "We won't be long." She pulled a candy bar from her purse and began to munch.

Lenora and the chauffeur exchanged sympathetic eye rolls as the nanny marched up the steps (the nanny chomping on her candy bar as they passed a NO FOOD IN THE LIBRARY sign) with Lenora in tow. But she was only in tow at first, then gradually less so as they climbed the stairs. By the time they reached the front desk, she had gotten herself completely out of tow. At that point it was easy to slip away.

She raced down one row of shelves and then another, putting distance between herself and the nanny before she could make a beeline for the children's section. Lenora loved the children's section. She loved libraries and being surrounded by silence and people reading. She threw her arms wide and inhaled deeply. This particular library was very new and did not smell enough like books yet to suit Lenora. But it did have lovely, large windows through which sunlight poured in eagerly, and beautiful cedar beams that stretched up to the high ceiling. Her parents hardly ever brought her here, and Lenora was determined, when she grew up, to go to the library anytime she wanted.

Her evasive route took her around the long way. She was in a section with books on philosophy (*I'll read those when I'm older,* she thought) and then books on math (she adored math but wasn't here for that today). She turned down a row she was certain led to the children's section, but instead it turned into a room full of books in a foreign language. She ran back and ended up surrounded by poetry. She flew past history and theater and hung a left at biology. The children's section was nowhere to be found. Instead the stacks and shelves seemed to get taller and taller and the rows longer and twistier.

She was lost. This gave her a jolt of pleasure.

As she stood contemplating everything she knew about how to escape from mazes (you could try taking every right-hand turn, for example), she suddenly heard voices. She rounded a corner and found a younger boy trying to get into a small room full of complex-looking books on astrophysics. But a man blocked his way.

The man had a fat, purplish face and looked quite angry. His head was jammed into a bowler hat and his body was wrapped in a too-tight overcoat, quite odd for a warm summer day. On his coat was a badge that said LIBARIAN. "You can't go in there," he told the boy.

"But I just want to see," pleaded the boy.

"You are far too young for those books. You wouldn't understand them. Besides, they're full of lies. Now go away!"

Lenora spoke up. "Really? They're all lies? Then why are they in the library?"

The man's head turned slowly toward Lenora. The rest of his body was perfectly still. Then something moved under his overcoat, like a snake wriggling across his stomach. She felt a tremor inside and took a step back.

"They won't be for long," the man said softly, his eyes narrowing. "I'll be removing them soon."

Lenora gulped, then looked at the boy, who was gazing at her with hope. "But you're not even a librarian," she said to the man, her voice hardly shaking at all.

"Of course I am," the man murmured. Lenora thought something flickered behind his eyes. He pointed at his badge.

"That's *not* how you spell *librarian*," said Lenora.

The man's eyes flickered again, like a snake's tongue. "It's an alternative spelling."

"I'm going to find a real librarian," replied Lenora, taking the boy by the hand and turning away. Partly she wanted to find a real librarian, and partly she wanted to get away from this man as quickly as possible. But then she heard a rush of air, and when she turned back, the man in the bowler hat was nowhere to be seen.

The boy looked up at Lenora. "What should I do?"

Lenora was resolute. "You should go on in and read whatever books you like."

"But the man said I was too young, and the books are all lies."

"Hmm," said Lenora. "A real librarian wouldn't tell you something like that. I think if a librarian *were* here, she would tell you to go in."

"Really?" said the boy, gazing at Lenora with wide eyes. "Are you sure?"

"Yep. Go!"

The boy dashed off happily and was soon immersed in a book on Einstein's gravitational lenses. Satisfied, Lenora returned to thoughts about alerting a real librarian to the man's presence and also finding the children's section before the nanny could chase her down.

Boom! Crack!

A great thundering, like a granite boulder splitting open, startled Lenora. It echoed from the direction she'd just come.

Curious, she went to see what it was. And it was something that Lenora was sure hadn't been there before. Where there had been a regular, blank wall, there was now a towering wall of old stone. Into it was carved an enormous archway. Above it, a phrase had been deeply chiseled:

KNOWLEDGE IS A LIGHT

Lenora's skin prickled at the words.

She stepped forward cautiously. The hall beyond the arch curved away into darkness. She couldn't see where it led. But she could smell something wonderful—the scent of many old books, a musty and thrilling odor, the sort of thing you would love to sniff if you poked your head up into an unfamiliar attic. And she could hear sounds, clacking and squeaking, but nothing she could identify.

Her heart pounded. Beyond this arch lay something she had never seen before, something new. If the nanny were here, she would order Lenora to turn back immediately.

Lenora stepped through the arch.

CHAPTER TWO

Lenora Enters
the Library

Lenora crept through the dark, running a hand over the cool, weathered stone. The exhilarating smell of old books got stronger. Soon she noticed a glow ahead of her and heard the murmur of many echoing voices. Lenora walked faster and the light grew brighter, and then she could see the end of the tunnel ahead, and an immense stone bridge beyond. She began to run and emerged onto the bridge, nearly falling to her knees.

The bridge spanned a vast, round tower. On either side of Lenora, two soaring walls of books curved around to meet again in the distance, on the faraway end of the bridge. All along the walls were hundreds of those rolling ladders people use to reach tall bookshelves. The ladders clacked and squeaked, sliding along busily, with librarians climbing up and down them and plucking books from the shelves or putting them back. They were coming in and out of doors, thousands of doors, set in stone walls between the unending shelves. Here and there were broad balconies with librarians hurrying along past circular windows the size of Ferris wheels, their arms full of books. None of them took any notice of Lenora as she gazed at all this in astonishment.

She threw back her head. The shelves rose higher than the eye could see. Sunlight beamed in from more giant windows set haphazardly in the walls. There were more bridges, too, like the one she was on, arching gracefully between the walls in all directions. She could see round shapes floating past the shelves, too far away to make out exactly, but they reminded her of balloons.

Gathering herself, she trotted to a railing and leaned over to look down. There was no end to the walls below, either, but she could see more stone bridges, down and down, with specks crossing the lowest ones that must be other people. She staggered back dizzily as a blimp rose into view, with an elegant wooden cabin attached beneath. Through its portholes she could see it was full of bookshelves, too. A librarian navigated the blimp by a wheel like a sailing ship's mounted at the helm.

Lenora walked a little farther along the bridge, until she got to a place where she could have a good look through one of the gigantic round windows in the tower's walls. She saw the outside walls of several more towers—like the one she was in, she supposed—and besides those, the tops of all kinds of other buildings, like pyramids and stately, columned edifices that looked like . . . like . . . well, she couldn't recall the name, but it was a building on a hill in Greece. All these were closely connected by bridges and webs of strange glass tubes through which dark shapes—she couldn't tell what from this far away—sped along.

She was trying to make sense of this startling view when motion at the other end of the bridge caught her eye. A thin, very tall librarian with dark skin was striding through the opposite archway. The woman came swiftly toward Lenora and soon was towering over her. "You!" the woman said, pointing down. "You are not allowed in this part of the library!"

Lenora leaned back to look up at her. The woman was at least ten feet tall, and she wore tall heels and carried a load of books under one arm. Everything about her was thin and sharp, from the sharp tips of her high heels to the point at the end of her nose. There were even two sharpened pencils thrust through the perfect bun of brown hair on top of her head. Her lips were pursed and she looked very stern.

"Why aren't I allowed?" asked Lenora.

"Because," the librarian replied, "you don't

work here. You're only allowed in this part of the library if you work here."

Lenora thought about the nanny and shopping and the unending boredom that lay ahead of her in the back of that limo. "Can I have a job, then?"

The librarian eyed Lenora carefully. "Tell me— how did you even get in here?"

"There was a loud crack, and an archway appeared." Lenora gestured over her shoulder. "And I just walked in."

The librarian raised her eyebrows ever so slightly. "I see." She looked at the arch, then back at Lenora. And after a moment's thought, she asked, "Do you swear to follow the librarian's oath? Do you swear to work hard? Do you swear to venture forth bravely and find the answer to any question, no matter the challenge?"

Lenora stood straight as an arrow. "I do."

The librarian drew herself up even taller. "Do you swear to find a path for those who are lost, and to improvise and think on your feet and rely on your wits and valor?"

Lenora couldn't help but hop up and down with excitement. "I do! I do!"

"And," said the librarian, fixing Lenora with a severe stare, "do you swear to oppose the enemies of knowledge with all your courage and strength, wherever they might be found?"

Lenora ceased her hopping. That last part sounded like the most serious promise of all. "I do so swear," she said solemnly.

"Then you're hired," said the librarian. "Come along."

CHAPTER THREE
Lenora Takes Over

Lenora trailed after the immensely tall librarian. She seemed to be steeped in authority, and as other librarians passed by they bowed their heads in respect. Though Lenora was used to being short herself, next to this woman she felt positively miniature. Together, the librarian and Lenora went through the archway on the opposite end of the bridge, leaving behind the bustling tower of books. Lenora turned around for one last look at the spectacle.

"Come along, Lenora," the librarian said. "There's no time to waste in this job."

Lenora came along. She wanted to make a good impression on her first day at work. "How do you know my name?"

"It is on your badge," came the prim reply.

Lenora looked down. On her chest, right in front of her heart, there was a small and exquisite name badge.

LENORA

—◦┊◦—

FOURTH ASSISTANT APPRENTICE LIBRARIAN

The badge made Lenora feel very professional, though she was nervous about the Fourth Assistant Apprentice part. It sounded like a rather lowly position, and she sensed she'd need to work hard to move up.

They were in a stately, stone-walled hallway now, big as a subway station and lined with carts covered with jumbled loads of books. Librarians hurried by, pushing more carts, bowing their heads at the woman. Everything was lit by huge sky-lights overhead. Lenora ran ahead to peer at the tall librarian's badge. The woman took very long strides, and Lenora had to march double-time just to keep up. She peered at the badge far above her.

MALACHI

CHIEF ANSWERER

Lenora was impressed. She wondered if she had what it took to be Chief Answerer someday. "Malachi," she said. "That's an odd name for a woman."

"Indeed," replied Malachi. "Very." She seemed to be thinking hard. "I'm trying to decide where to place you, Lenora. Tell me, what happened in Spain on October 5, 1582?"

Lenora was crestfallen. "I don't know," she confessed. Her first question, and she had already failed.

"Then we'll start you off at the Help Desk for calendars," Malachi said. "You'll be answering any and all calendar-related questions."

"But wouldn't it make more sense for me to work on things I already know about?" Lenora asked.

"Not at all!" Malachi arched one eyebrow. "Whyever would you want to do THAT? You'd learn absolutely nothing!"

Lenora supposed Malachi had a point. If she never had to answer questions about things she didn't know, she'd never get better at her job. She'd be a Fourth Assistant Apprentice all her life. Horrifying visions of her gray-haired self plodding these halls as an elderly Fourth Assistant were interrupted as they emerged from the hallway into a corridor as long as the previous room had been tall. It was like a subway tunnel, but ten times as big. All along it in both directions sailed balloons of all colors. Stacks of books tied with string dangled from them. Lenora gawked at this as Malachi hurried her along to the left and down a spiral staircase.

"May I ask a question?" asked Lenora, panting a bit from the hurry.

"Always," came the crisp reply.

"There were words above that archway I came through—'Knowledge Is a Light.'"

"Yes, there would have been. And as a curious librarian, you are wondering what they meant."

"Oh . . . yes!" said Lenora, wondering just how many of her thoughts Malachi knew.

"It would be best if you figured that out for yourself, Lenora," Malachi said, and nothing more.

Lenora thought about the words as they clomped down the stairs. At the bottom, they came to another archway. This one had the word CALENDARS carved above it. Inside was a giant room, completely square. Lenora thought an entire mansion could fit in this one room. All over the walls were calendars. In the middle of the room was a desk with a big sign in front that read HELP DESK.

"Here is your desk," said Malachi. "When a patron comes to your desk, say, 'Hello. How may I help you?' You'll figure out the rest from there." Before Lenora could reply, Malachi hurried away.

Lenora was alone. She looked at the walls. Calendars for every year seemed to be here, covered in notes and reminders. She saw 1953 and 809 and even 2056 and 3.

Her heart thumped with excitement. Her own desk at her own job! She looked around. She supposed she could lay claim to this entire room as well. Then she realized that a patron could come along with a question at any time, and she knew nothing about calendars. It was time to get started. Fumbling through her pockets, she found a hair tie and pulled her black locks back into a ponytail, then went behind her desk, where she saw a padded stool and a bookshelf. She looked over the books. The first one she noticed was a dictionary. She picked it up and flipped to *W*.

She ran her finger down the pages, looking for

whyever. Malachi had used that word, but Lenora had never heard it before.

But the word wasn't there. Lenora did not think this was fair. *Whenever* was a word. So were *whoever, whichever, whatever,* and even *however.* This was a situation that had to be corrected. Taking a pen from a cup on her desk, she wrote carefully between *whydah* and *why'll*:

WHY•EV•ER: meaning "for what reason, as in 'Whyever would anyone not want to learn new things?'"

Satisfied, she replaced the dictionary and looked for a book that might help her learn more about calendars. She was not surprised to see a book titled *Everything, and I Mean Everything, You Might Ever Want to Know About Calendars.* This was the Calendars Help Desk, after all. She began to read. She became completely absorbed. Calendars were much more interesting than she would ever have imagined. She read and read, learning many new things. For example, she learned the answer to what happened in Spain on October 5, 1582: absolutely nothing at all. Nothing happened on October 5, 1582, in Spain, and that was because—

She was interrupted by someone clearing their throat.

She looked up. In front of the Help Desk stood a very advanced-looking robot. It looked like a handsome older gentleman in a well-tailored suit, with shiny metal skin and blinking red lights for eyes and an inquisitive expression on its face. This was a robot with a question.

Lenora felt her mouth go dry. The robot looked serious and intelligent. Lenora wondered how she could ever be of assistance to such a sophisticated being. She took a deep breath, thought, *One step at a time,* and remembered what Malachi had told her to do.

"Hello," said Lenora. "How may I help you?"

"Hello," said the robot. It had a natural voice that didn't sound robotic at all. "My name is

Bendigeidfran. I was sent by the King of Starpoint Seventeen."

"Never heard of it," said Lenora.

"It is located in what is called the Great Rift Valley in your time," the robot explained. "I come from the year 8000."

"Interesting," replied Lenora. She realized she ought to be taking notes. She found a box in one drawer that read NOTEBOOKS—WATERPROOF AND FIREPROOF. She removed one of the pads. *In the year 8000,* she wrote, *the Kingdom of Starpoint Seventeen is located in Great Rift Valley.*

"Ben-di-geid-fran," she pronounced carefully. "That is a rather long name."

"Thank you," Bendigeidfran said. "It's Welsh. Some things in Wales have quite long names."

Lenora added this to her notes.

The robot continued, "I was sent here by my king, because the kingdom is in chaos, even more so than usual."

"Why is the kingdom usually in chaos?"

"Because the people of the Kingdom of Starpoint

Seventeen are a little . . ." The robot hesitated. "Well, you'll see. We need a librarian, and the king says she must appear before him personally. He needs to appear to be in control of the situation."

"I understand completely," said Lenora. It was important to appear in control of the situation, but even more important to actually be in control of the situation, and to be in control of the situation you needed to know the facts. And Lenora knew the facts. Or at least some of them. She knew she had much to learn. But she remembered the words of her oath, her promise to venture forth bravely and find the answer to any question, and she knew it was time to put herself to the test.

"Take me to your king," said Lenora. "I assume you've got a time machine somewhere."

"Right here," said Bendigeidfran, and he pointed at his wrist. There was a device there Lenora would have called a watch, but she supposed in 8000 those could double as time machines. "Ready?"

"One question before we go," said Lenora.

"Why did you come to me? Aren't there libraries in 8000?"

"Of course," said the robot. "But there was a bit of a line."

He touched his time machine and they both vanished.

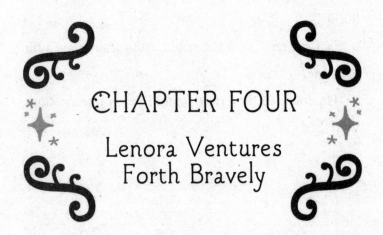

CHAPTER FOUR

Lenora Ventures Forth Bravely

At least, Lenora assumed she and the robot had vanished from the Calendar room. Because they certainly weren't in the library anymore. They were in front of an enormous pair of marble doors in a wide courtyard open to the sky. The courtyard was covered in smooth white tiles. Everything around them was peaceful and quiet. There was no chaos in sight. Lenora's gaze traveled up to the open sky. There she saw giant red letters blinking: ERROR, the letters said, over and over.

"What is that?" asked Lenora, pointing.

The robot looked just as puzzled. "I don't remember. I'm sure it's the reason for the chaos, though."

"You don't remember? Robots have memory banks, don't they?" She thought she had seen that in a movie somewhere.

"Yes, but . . ." Bendigeidfran hesitated. "I've been having problems with my memory unit ever since I bashed my head against the nose of the Great Sphinx of Giza." He pointed to a dent next to a small panel on his metal head. "Maybe you could take a look?"

"I suppose you'd want a librarian from the Robotics section for that," said Lenora. "But it can't hurt to try. Open up."

The robot knelt and pressed on the panel, which popped open. Lenora peered inside. As she expected, much about a robotic brain from the year 8000 meant absolutely nothing to her. But amid all the dancing lights and graceful whirling dials she noticed a spot with six slots on it. The trouble was, only five of those spots were occupied by glittering chips. The sixth slot was empty.

"Do you suppose you are missing a chip?" she said. "It could have gotten knocked off when you bashed your head."

The robot snapped his fingers as his eyes changed to a happy green. "Yes! That must be it. I'll have to go back and find it. But first—we must do something about the chaos."

"Of course," said Lenora. "But I don't see any signs of chaos."

"You will," Bendigeidfran replied. He threw open the doors.

They were staring down a wide, ornate hall with many interesting details. But Lenora couldn't notice any of them because of the chaos. It was exactly as you would expect chaos to be. People were running up and down and back and forth, screaming or muttering or both. Some of them threw their hands in the air, while others hugged themselves and shuddered. Their clothes could have been called strange, but Lenora had every expectation that people in 8000 would dress differently, so this did not surprise her. She was well prepared for time travel.

"The librarian is here!" cried Bendigeidfran. "Make way for the librarian!"

The panicking people threw themselves against the sides of the hall, clearing a path for Lenora. She strode down the hall beside Bendigeidfran, hoping desperately that the robot's trust in her was not misplaced. After all, it was only her first day on the job.

"Save us, librarian!" a pale-faced man whimpered.

Lenora tried to think of what Malachi might say. Malachi, she decided, would surely appear to be in control of the situation. "Do not fear. All will be well," Lenora said to the man, both to comfort him and also herself. He smiled at her in relief.

Now she could see some of the details of the hall. The main one was the statue. It was really a set of statues, all copies of the same sculpture, and there were hundreds of them lining the hall. The statues were all of a small boy, a few years younger than Lenora, with a rather large head and a pair of owlish glasses. He looked solemn and confident.

Soon Lenora and Bendigeidfran were approaching another set of huge marble doors. These doors were attended by a bunch of men in fancy, frilly coats who began blowing trumpets as the pair neared. When they paused at the doors, the trumpeting ceased and the men bowed to Lenora. Behind her, the crowd in the hall applauded wildly. Lenora didn't find any of this to be necessary at all, and she wondered if the Kingdom of Starpoint Seventeen wasn't overdoing things just a bit.

"Before we go in," Bendigeidfran whispered, "I should warn you. Not everyone is happy you are here. The Court Historian and Court Mathematician believe they have all the answers, and they told the king there was no need for a librarian at all. Be wary of both of them."

Lenora gulped, then reminded herself that she had promised to think on her feet and improvise and rely on her wits and valor. She just wished the moment for that hadn't come quite so quickly.

The men in frilly coats pushed open the doors, and together she and the robot entered the throne room. Lenora knew it was the throne room because there was a throne in it. On it sat, unsurprisingly, a small boy with a large head and a pair of owlish glasses. He looked solemn and confident. Lenora wondered if he was actually panicking inside. On one side of him stood a man who looked very much like a court historian and, on the other, a woman who looked exactly like a court mathematician. The mass of people from the hall flowed into the throne room and stood all around, murmuring.

All eyes were on Lenora.

The throne room was open to the sky. ERROR, blinked the letters there.

"Hello, Your Majesty," said Lenora. "How may I help you?"

"You mayn't!" snarled the Court Historian at the same time the Court Mathematician barked, "No need!"

"Ahem!" said the king, and both went quiet, glaring at Lenora. The king gave them a look of admonishment and addressed her. "Centuries ago, our scientists put a giant calendar on a screen in the sky, so everyone in the kingdom would always know what day it was. We got so used to it that we forgot how to tell the dates ourselves. Then yesterday, at midnight, the error message suddenly appeared. Now no one knows what day it is, and my kingdom is on the verge of collapse."

"Well," said Lenora, after a moment's thought, "what day was it yesterday?"

The crowd murmured again. Lenora wished they would stop doing that.

The King of Starpoint Seventeen's brow furrowed. It was a tiny, almost imperceptible furrow. "I really don't know," he said, in the voice of a small, ever so slightly unconfident boy. "It's embarrassing, I admit. But we never had to bother remembering before. The screen just told us." He gestured toward a sweating, nervous-looking man in the corner. "My court scientist is prepared to reset the calendar and save my kingdom, but he can't do that until we know the date."

Lenora turned to Bendigeidfran. "Any chance that's in one of the memory chips you've still got?"

The crowd gasped.

"Maybe, but . . ." The robot hesitated. "I have been getting extra confused on dates in particular."

"Think hard," said Lenora encouragingly.

Bendigeidfran thought hard. His eyes went an intense purple. Finally, he replied, "I think . . . it might have been February 28, 8000."

"Right!" gasped the king. He looked relieved. "I remember now!"

"Excuse me," sniffed the Court Historian. "As Your Majesty knows, I went to the history books right away when the error message appeared. And if yesterday was February 28, then it is clear that today should be February 29." He peered down his nose at Lenora. She wondered if his authority felt threatened. "As I told you, Your Majesty, we didn't need a librarian at all!"

Lenora began to get a feeling. She'd just been

reading about this in her book. "Why do you think it is February 29?"

"Because," sighed the Court Historian, rolling his eyes, "according to ancient records from the year 5739, there's something called a leap year in any year that can be divided by four. In a leap year, the date goes from February twenty-eighth to the twenty-ninth!"

"8000 can be divided by four," piped up the Court Mathematician. "We hardly need a librarian to determine THAT!"

Lenora's feeling became a theory. She was about to speak when the king interrupted.

"Then it is settled!" he cried. "Reset the calendar!"

The Court Scientist grasped a lever in a wall nearby.

For an instant, Lenora hesitated. Everyone in the court seemed so sure of themselves. But she had a theory, and she knew she must be brave, or disaster would surely follow.

"Wait!" she shouted. "Stop!"

CHAPTER FIVE
Lenora Saves the Day

The throne room's hysterical crowd erupted with shouts and cries. The Court Scientist released the lever and looked at the king.

Lenora tried to continue speaking but couldn't hear herself or anything else over the crowd's bedlam. She whirled to face them. "Everyone—please *SHUSH*!"

Instantly, the crowd went dead silent and looked wide-eyed at Lenora. She felt a little guilty, but really, a librarian had a right to a bit of silence when needed.

She turned to the king. "It isn't February 29, Your Majesty," she said. "It's March 1!"

The Court Mathematician smirked. "Wrong, librarian. The math proves it."

Muffled gasps from the crowd.

"No, the history proves it!" exclaimed the Court Historian.

More gasps, and Lenora looked around to see everyone on the tips of their toes, leaning forward, awaiting her response. Her mind raced with the facts she had read in the calendar book. "Neither one proves it alone," she said carefully. "You have to take both together. Leap years don't always come every four years. According to the rules, century years, like 1800 and 1900, are not leap years. But they—"

"This is a century year," interrupted the Court Historian. "It's 8000. Make up your mind!"

"As I was about to say," Lenora said, determined to be patient and professional, "that rule switches every four hundred years. 1600 and 2000, for example, were both leap years."

"Fine!" said the Court Mathematician rudely. "The math still says 8000 is one of those years."

"Not quite," said Lenora, pointing a finger to the sky as she reached her dramatic conclusion. "There is something the scientists who built the screen must not have known. By the year 4000 the calendar would have been off by a day, unless they added a rule that switches things every 4000 years. And that means 8000, like 4000 and 12000, must be a common year."

"I assume," mused the king, "that a common year is anything that is not a leap year."

"Correct," said Lenora.

"Clearly, this librarian knows her calendars." The king looked at his mathematician and historian, who appeared rather ashamed of themselves and were staring studiously at their toes. "If there are no objections, we shall reset the date to March 1."

Relief flooded Lenora. But at the same time, she

felt that something was still wrong. They had yet to solve the real problem. She could see herself returning here in 12000 and then 16000 and on and on to solve the exact same problem every time. "Pardon me, Your Majesty," she said, "but I don't think you should reset the screen. I think you should take it down."

"Whyever would we do that?" asked the king in surprise.

"Because," said Lenora, "you don't want to depend on the screen, do you? It will just mean more confusion every four thousand years."

"Very wise," said the king. He turned to the Court Scientist. "Bring down the screen," he ordered. "From this day forward, we will learn to tell dates ourselves!"

There was general cheering. This time, Lenora didn't shush the crowd. In the midst of the celebration, the king approached Lenora with a laurel wreath and placed it on her head. "You have served me well. I hereby appoint you my Court Librarian!"

The roars grew louder. Lenora felt a humming just above her heart. She looked down at her badge.

LENORA

———— ·:· ————

THIRD ASSISTANT APPRENTICE LIBRARIAN

OFFICIAL COURT LIBRARIAN OF THE KINGDOM

OF STARPOINT SEVENTEEN

Third Assistant! thought Lenora happily. Only her first day at her job, and she'd already been promoted. Which reminded her—she really must get back to the Help Desk. She looked about for Bendigeidfran and saw that he had been pulled into a corner by a short elderly woman with dour features and a too-tight overcoat and a black bowler hat jammed onto her head. She was whispering into the robot's ear and glancing at Lenora.

Lenora started toward the pair, then stopped. Her arm was suddenly covered in goose bumps.

The woman in the too-tight overcoat and bowler hat reminded her very much of the man she'd encountered outside the Astrophysics room at the library back home, and she chilled Lenora through and through. Though she had a badge saying LIBRARIAN (spelled correctly this time), Lenora could not imagine what business she had in the court of the King of Starpoint Seventeen.

The woman glanced again at Lenora. For a moment, their gazes locked, and something behind her eyes flickered. Twice. And across her shoulders, something slithered beneath the overcoat. Lenora, to her shame, froze on the spot. The woman spoke to Bendigeidfran for a moment longer, then patted him on the back and trotted down a narrow corridor and out of sight.

Gathering herself, and furious that the woman had frightened her even for a moment, Lenora went to Bendigeidfran. "Who was that?"

"I must say, your boss there is an extremely curious librarian," said the robot.

"What?" asked Lenora, outraged. That woman

was not her boss. Or was she? Lenora didn't really know much about how the library worked yet. But she was certain that Malachi would have told her about this woman. And Lenora really, really, really did not believe she was a librarian, whatever her badge might say.

Thinking these things, she wasn't really listening as Bendigeidfran told her the woman said there was an emergency in Lenora's section, and she should return immediately.

By the time the robot's words sank in for Lenora, he was already reaching for the time machine on his wrist. "When was it that I got you? Ah yes, she instructed me very specifically—October 5, 1582!" He touched the device.

"NO!" shouted Lenora. She grabbed for the time machine. But it was too late.

She found herself tumbling through a dark void, Bendigeidfran spinning beside her. All around them was nothingness, stretching on forever, and somewhere in the far distance was a faint but growing rumbling.

"What happened!?" cried the robot.

"There *was* no October 5, 1582," said Lenora. The woman in the bowler hat had done this on purpose, it was clear, and Lenora was sure she would soon find out why. There were still goose bumps on her arm, and a fluttering sense in her stomach that peril was near. And that rumbling was turning into a roar.

"But how can that be?" said Bendigeidfran.

"Because the ancient Romans got the length of the year wrong," said Lenora, her eyes darting about for the danger she was sure would crop up at any moment. "They were eleven minutes off. By 1582, things had gotten so messed up that the pope had to start a new calendar entirely and skip ten days while he was at it. You know, I really think we should get out of here."

"Agreed," said the robot. He touched the device. But nothing happened, and his eyes began to blink in crimson alarm.

"What's wrong?" asked Lenora with dread.

"The void seems to be draining power from my

time machine," Bendigeidfran said. "I've got almost nothing left."

"What does that mean?" asked Lenora. "How do we get out without your time machine?"

The robot shook his head. "We don't. I'm afraid we're lost in time and space forever, Lenora. Well, not forever. That roar you hear"—which the robot was now having to shout over—"is the void reacting to the presence of matter, by which I mean us! Eventually it will rip us up into nothing, too."

Lenora didn't like the sound of that. The roar was now a howling. Her skin tingled. She looked down at her arm and saw it was fading into nothing. She looked at Bendigeidfran. He was fading into nothing, too.

"I'm sorry," shouted Bendigeidfran over the deafening howl. "This is all my fault!"

"No time for that," yelled Lenora. The howl was making her skull rattle, and Lenora could barely see Bendigeidfran, or herself. She thought quickly. "You said your time machine had *almost* nothing left. Does that mean it has a little left?"

"Yes!" cried the robot. "But almost nothing! We'd never get back to your real time."

"We don't have to!" screamed Lenora over the din. Her arm was only a dim outline now, and she could barely see Bendigeidfran. "There *was* an October 4! Is there enough power to move just one day?"

The robot's eyes flashed faintly, and he grasped desperately at his wrist.

Suddenly, they were standing in a dark forest, the ground covered with an early snow. In front of them stood a girl in a yellow cloak, her arms full of firewood. Her jaw dropped and so did the wood.

"Power restored!" said Bendigeidfran happily.

"Pardon us," said Lenora to the girl. "But we must be leaving. Here," she said to the robot, who was reaching for his wrist. "You'd better let me do that." She entered the date herself, and in moments they were back at the Help Desk in the Calendars section. Lenora collapsed onto her padded stool in weary relief.

"My apologies, Lenora," said the robot, his eyes

now blinking a sad blue. "I should not have listened to that strange woman."

Lenora stroked his hand reassuringly. "All is well. I made it home. And you could not have known she was lying."

"Still," said Bendigeidfran, "you should be careful, Lenora. It seems you have an enemy."

"I will," replied Lenora, wondering who the woman in the bowler hat was, and if she would be seeing her or the other man again. She rather suspected she would.

"As for me," said Bendigeidfran, bowing deeply, "you have saved the kingdom and both our lives. I am truly impressed and grateful. Tell me, would you consider voyaging through time with me, running errands for the king? It's rather interesting work. My next assignment is to see whether the Battle of Pelusium was really fought with cats."

For a moment, Lenora was tempted, imagining all the wonderful times she could visit alongside her new friend. Then she looked around at the Calendars section, and her heart fluttered to think of all that lay ahead of her in the library. "Maybe later," she said. "I can't just abandon my job like that. I have a lot of responsibilities. And I love the work." Even if it did strand her in time and space now and then.

"I understand," said the robot. "Perhaps we shall meet again. Now I must return home as well."

"Wait," said Lenora. "Don't you think you should go find your missing chip first? I have a feeling you'll get in all sorts of trouble if you don't."

"Of course!" said the robot. "Where was it again?"

"Ancient Egypt. The Sphinx. You bashed your head . . ."

"Right!" exclaimed the robot, reaching for his wrist. In a flash he was gone.

And in his place stood Malachi.

CHAPTER SIX

Lenora Takes to the Skies

Malachi read aloud from Lenora's badge. "Third Assistant Apprentice already, I see. You have done well, Lenora." The corner of the Chief Answerer's mouth almost twitched into a smile. "But you mustn't be content to rest on your laurels. We have a problem, and I think you might be just the one to solve it. The librarian in our Cartography section has quit in a huff, and on the worst day possible. We just got a brand-new globe delivered, and huge crowds have come to see it."

"It must be some globe!" Lenora said, impressed.

"Indeed," said Malachi. "And there is no one there to answer their questions. The Help Desk is swamped. This will be a challenging assignment. Do you think you can manage it?"

"Yes," replied Lenora instantly, though in her heart she was not quite sure.

"Excellent," said Malachi. "Follow me." They left Calendars and went into the hallway. They soon came to a platform from which stairs wound off in all directions, up and down. They hurried down some steps, up some steps (Lenora had completely lost her way at this point—she thought the maze of stairways could use a few signs), and tiptoed through a vast reading room in which hundreds of people were studiously bent over books in perfect silence. Lenora looked at all the people reading and learning, and thought about the words *Knowledge Is a Light* and what they might mean. She remembered Starpoint Seventeen's giant glowing calendar in the sky and wondered if the phrase meant that knowledge is like the sun in the sky, shining down on everything. But no, that didn't seem quite right somehow . . .

She continued to ponder this as they left the reading room and found themselves in another large hallway lined with bookshelves. They passed two rooms that appeared to be completely empty. Above the first was a sign: SHRINKING ROOM. Librarians were going into it but none were coming out. The other was the UNSHRINKING ROOM, and it was just the opposite.

"What are those for?" asked Lenora.

"Some of our patrons are very small," replied Malachi. She came to a halt at the end of the hallway, where it formed a T with another hallway, equally large, along which an enormous stream of library patrons was hurrying. "You can find your way from here. Simply follow the crowd." With that, she whirled away and was gone.

Cartography was not difficult to find. Everyone was flowing in the same direction, talking excitedly about the new globe. Children were pulling their parents along by the hand. Soon they were rushing down a set of wide, sweeping steps and then across a bridge that arched over a brook of babbling water.

Lenora paused (briefly, because she knew Cartography needed her) for a look. At the other end of the bridge, where the hallway resumed, was a set of steps going down to a dock with several empty canoes. The brook had the most inviting grassy banks (Lenora assumed they somehow got enough sun from the skylights above), and it curved under the bridge before going around a bend. Down the brook, patrons were paddling canoes. A sign on the dock said HYDROLOGY, with an arrow pointing downstream. Lenora was tempted to grab a paddle and voyage off. But she had a job to do. The scientific study of the movement of water on Earth and other planets would have to wait for another time.

She reached Cartography and gasped.

The room was far bigger than any room Lenora had ever seen. All along the walls, going up and up, were thousands of maps of every possible description. Patrons were walking about on walkways, stairs, and ramps, studying the maps. Far, far above what must have been miles of maps and walkways was the hint of a ceiling hung with twinkling lights. A journey across this room would be no small undertaking. But even this space was nearly filled by its simply magnificent globe, which could really be described as a small world, floating with great dignity in the center of the room and rotating slowly.

There was a huge sign beneath it: WORLD'S LARGEST GLOBE.

Underneath, in smaller letters, it said RAISED RELIEF.

Lenora hardly had time to admire any of this. She spotted the Help Desk right away, with a long line of desperate-looking questioners waving library cards and shuffling impatiently. She hurried over, having no doubt the line might move a little faster if only the globe were a little smaller. How could she be expected to make use of such a globe when she couldn't even reach it?

She soon found the answer. Behind the Help Desk bobbed a gas balloon, with a basket beneath it into which one librarian could nicely fit. It drifted back and forth, tugging at a rope that anchored it to the floor. A small set of steps led up to the basket. Next to the steps was a sign: LIBRARIANS ONLY.

She felt a tug at her arm. It was a forlorn-looking young man with a tricorne hat in his hand. Sadness and regret came off him in waves.

"Hello," said Lenora. "How may I help you?" And she did really want to help this poor, sad man.

"P-P-Please, librarian," stammered the patron, turning the hat in his hands. "There was a girl I loved, and I never told her. Now she has moved far away, and I want to tell her, but I don't know where to send the letter. All I know is that she moved to the place with the longest name in the world. And I don't know where that is."

Lenora pondered this. She didn't know, either. But it was her job to find out. She looked around, but none of the maps in her vicinity looked like they would help with this question.

She turned toward the gas balloon with great trepidation. She had absolutely no idea how to work a gas balloon, particularly not this one, which had attachments like sails and wings connected to ropes connected to dozens of levers on a control board in the basket. It looked unimaginably complicated. She searched for instructions but couldn't find a thing. *No wonder the previous librarian quit in a huff!* thought Lenora. But there was nothing for it. She certainly wasn't quitting the best job she'd ever had. She had to figure it out.

She climbed aboard. Terms connected to balloons, like *ballast* and *envelope*, went through her head, but she had no idea what they meant. She tried to sort through the levers, none of which bothered with helpful things like labels or directions. She found one that was connected to the rope anchoring the balloon to the floor. She gave it a hopeful pull, and in an instant the balloon shot up into the air and the Help Desk dwindled away below.

A strange thing happened as Lenora got closer to the orb. Gravity simply switched from the Earth to the globe. The balloon rotated until the globe was no longer above her, but below. Now she was soaring over a blue ocean, and then along a coastline, with the floor and walls of the Cartography section forming the sky. She was astonished to see, below her, a school of fish swimming by, ignoring her completely.

The balloon was going faster and faster. The ocean rocketed by. The coastline blurred past. Lenora pulled desperately at the levers as wings flapped and sails unfurled. She was thrown back and forth in the basket as the balloon jerked about wildly, completely out of control. *This will never work,* thought Lenora. She wasn't sure that whoever built this balloon was really the right person for the job. But she would simply have to make the best of it. The balloon was proving useless, but she had to get an answer for that sad young man.

She searched and searched until she found one lever that lifted flaps that briefly brought the balloon to a lurching halt.

And then she clambered onto the edge of the basket, swayed for a moment, and jumped.

CHAPTER SEVEN
Lenora Sails the Seas

Lenora landed firmly on her feet along the rocky coastline of the world's largest globe. The out-of-control balloon careened away into the distance. *Good riddance,* she thought. She had grown to hate that balloon. Beyond it, in what was now the sky, she could see the Cartography section's wall of maps curving off to the horizon, its walkways with railings far out of reach.

Now, how to find the place with the longest name in the world? Unlike her experience in the Calendars section, Lenora had not had time to read a book on cartography. She was going to have to improvise and think on her feet and rely on her wits and valor. She remembered something Bendigeidfran had said. *Some things in Wales have quite long names.* Lenora supposed that was as good a place to start as any. But how could she find Wales?

As she stared out at the sea, thinking, she saw letters, large and black, floating on the waves. ATLANTIC OCEAN, they said. If everything on the globe was labeled, she ought to be able to track down Wales eventually. She just wished she had some idea where to start.

She hurried along the coast as ATLANTIC OCEAN floated off toward the equator. She looked and looked, searching . . . and then, not far from where the letters GULF OF SAINT LAWRENCE floated, she saw something in the water. A thrill went up her spine.

"Wow!" she shouted. "A group of whales!"

One of the whales turned and surfaced, huge

waves leaping up around it. It blew a huge spout of water into the air as it swam toward Lenora.

"Excuse me," the whale said huffily. "But we are not a *group*. We are a *pod*. It's not the same thing at all." The other whales, all of them perfectly white, swam up beside the first and made a cacophony of high-pitched whistles and squeaks.

Lenora could tell she had offended the whales. "I'm sorry," she said. "But do you mind if I ask you a question?"

The first whale puffed itself up rather happily and seemed to brighten all over. "Why," said the whale proudly, "a librarian wants to ask *me* a question? I am quite honored."

Lenora was glad she was forgiven. "I would like to know," she said, "how to find Wales."

"You've found them," said the whale. "We are, in fact, beluga whales."

"Oh," said Lenora. "I mean Wales, the place, not whales, the mammal."

"Hmph," replied the whale, and it blew another spout of water. "And I suppose you think that just because I am a whale, the mammal, that I automatically know the location of Wales, the place?"

Lenora reddened. Beluga whales seemed easily offended. "I'm sorry," she said. She began to turn away.

"Wait," said the whale. It sniffed, via blowhole. "As it happens, I have a cousin who once went on vacation off the coast of Wales. This is purely a coincidence, however."

"I understand," said Lenora.

"Since you are a librarian," the whale continued, "I can only assume your question is of the utmost importance. So, although my pod normally never leaves this estuary, I will make an exception and take you there straightaway. Hop on." The whale beckoned with one fin.

Lenora climbed aboard and the pod headed off straightaway. With strong swipes of their flukes, the whales cut through the ocean. Lenora staggered a bit until she got her sea legs, then planted herself forward in a comfortable spot behind the whale's adorably bulbous head, her gaze fixed on the horizon as waves parted around her and strong salty scents filled her nostrils. *This is so much better than a limousine,* she thought. "You speak excellent English," she remarked to the whale. "I didn't know whales could do that."

"Oh yes," said the whale airily. "Beluga whales have been known to mimic your speech. Unlike *regular* whales, we belugas have *exceptional* vocal mechanics. Generally we use them to play pranks."

Interesting, thought Lenora. She added this to her notebook: *Beluga whales mimic human speech. Jokes abound.*

Shortly afterward a pair of islands came into view. Waves crashed against rocky cliffs covered in green. Letters floated over the islands: IRELAND and ENGLAND. The pod plunged directly between the pair. And then Lenora saw it straight ahead: WALES.

The pod dropped her off on the coast. Lenora waved as they spouted their goodbyes, swimming away backward. "Good luck, librarian!" they cried. "May your waters always be filled with salmon!" They dove beneath the waves and were gone.

What remarkable creatures! thought Lenora. Even if they were a bit arrogant.

She searched all over Wales. She found lots of places, grassy hills and ruined castles and green fields and stone fences. Sheep were everywhere, some of them curiously painted with colorful spots. (*Painted sheep—why?* she scribbled in her notes.) But she did not find any names of particular length. She was almost ready to give up and search elsewhere when she came upon an island in the northwest corner of the country. It held a small town with a name so long the letters spilled over into the Irish Sea at both ends:

LLANFAIRPWLLGWYNGYLLGOGERYCHWYRNDROB-
WLLLLANTYSILIOGOGOGOCH

Underneath this was written in parentheses: (*LLAN-VIRE-POOLL-GUIN-GILL-GO-GER-U-QUEERN-DROB-OOLL-LLANDUS-ILIO-GOGO-GOCH*). *That* must *be it,* Lenora thought, and recorded this in her notebook.

Satisfied, she put her notebook under her arm. Time to get back to her desk. She looked up at the

Cartography section in the sky. Shelves, walkways, walls, desks, and maps were all far away and completely out of reach. And there was no sign of the runaway balloon anywhere. *Oh dear,* Lenora thought to herself with growing alarm.

She was trapped.

CHAPTER EIGHT
Lenora Travels the Globe

Lenora gazed longingly at a walkway in the sky. On the wall of the Cartography room beyond it, there was a world map, though the world on it looked nothing like Earth. The walkway had a railing that kept patrons from falling to their deaths. All the thousands of walkways zigzagging everywhere in the Cartography room had them. If she could only reach one of those railings, perhaps she could pull herself off the globe she was trapped on. But all of them looked to be far beyond her reach as they rotated past. As one walkway came into view, Lenora could see a startled young boy with an ice-cream cone gaping down . . . up?—she wasn't sure—at her.

"No ice cream in the library!" snapped Lenora, wagging her finger. Startled, the boy dropped the ice cream and ran away. Lenora sighed. She supposed she'd have to clean that up, if she could ever get off the globe. If only she were as tall as Malachi . . .

She snapped her fingers. *Of course!* She just needed to get to a higher spot! And everyone knows the highest point on Earth is Mount Everest. Maybe she could reach a walkway railing from there when one of them rotated by. But she was not entirely sure where Mount Everest was. She would just have to look.

She ran across England until she found herself at a strip of water—ENGLISH CHANNEL, it was labeled. She eyed the coast of France on the other side. Lenora took a few steps back for a running start.

With a leap, she was over the channel, almost. At least she didn't get any water above the ankles.

France flew by under her feet, then more of Europe. Her parents were sailing around down there somewhere on the real globe, she supposed. Without her. She gave Europe a little stomp and ran on. She ran down the boot-shaped country of Italy and came up short. Here was the Mediterranean Sea, and it was too much for her to leap over. But there was a rowboat conveniently docked on the nearby island of Sicily. She splashed over—her shoes were already wet so it didn't matter—and rowed away. She steered past the Rock of Gibraltar—which she'd always imagined was just a big rock but turned out to be a massive limestone fortress covered with monkeys—and north along the coast of Portugal with its blue-green waters. She saw mountains here and there, but none of them were Mount Everest.

On one of the mountains she spotted the balloon.

It had gotten itself wedged in a rocky outcrop

and was fighting desperately to break free. Propellers were whirling, flaps were flapping, and sails were pulling this way and that in the high mountain wind. Lenora paddled closer. Despite her loathing for the balloon, it could offer escape from the globe.

As she neared the coast, she spotted a dark figure on the other side of the balloon's basket.

A young, skinny man wearing a black bowler hat and an overcoat that was much too large for him.

He had an axe and was chopping away the part of the basket that was stuck in the rocks.

"Hey!" shouted Lenora, outraged. "That is library property!"

The man glanced in her direction, then gave a final chop, and the balloon soared free over the mountains, back toward Europe and far away from Lenora.

The man in the bowler hat hopped over the eastern edge of the mountain and was gone.

Lenora rowed away furiously, thinking hard about these people in overcoats and black bowler hats. The first had tried to keep that young boy from learning about astrophysics. The second had lied to Bendigeidfran, and she and the robot had almost been lost in time and space. The third had deliberately sabotaged the balloon that might have gotten her off this globe. Whoever these people were and whyever they were doing these things, Lenora had no idea, but she was determined to find out.

For now, she journeyed onward.

The air began to get rather cold as she paddled past Ireland and the jagged fjords of Norway. She shivered, realizing the North Pole must be somewhere ahead and the air would only get colder as she approached it. But she felt that she had seen a picture of Mount Everest covered in snow. Perhaps she should keep going. Dodging an iceberg, she noticed a group . . . pod? . . . pack? . . . of rather dismal-looking penguins milling about on an icy coast nearby. While she wanted to stop to admire them, she had a patron waiting for an answer. Steeling herself against the freezing air, she continued across the tossing and ice-strewn Arctic Ocean, looking for tall mountains.

Suddenly, she dug her oars into the water as a realization hit her. The rowboat bounced and swayed as she ground, or rather watered, to a halt.

Lenora might not have known much about cartography. But she did know penguins. And everyone who knows about penguins knows they live near the South Pole, not the North. Those dismal-looking penguins were far, far from home. She remembered the words of the Oath: *Do you swear to find a path for those who are lost?*

As a librarian, it was her job to help these castaway penguins, even if it meant a delay for another patron. She hauled on the oars until she was back facing the penguins on their little island. Soon she had rowed her way up to the bunch (group? pod? herd?) of confused-looking birds.

"Hello," said Lenora. "How may I help you?"

The penguins looked at her and flapped their wings in distress and made various honks and squeals, but nothing that Lenora could understand.

"Rats," said Lenora. She opened her notebook. *Penguins can't speak English,* she wrote. *Got lucky with the belugas.*

Then she noticed, beside the penguins, a half-opened cardboard box labeled FOR LIBRARIANS ONLY. She pulled open a flap. Inside, nestled amid foam packing peanuts, were several pairs of headphones, each with a mini-microphone. PENGUIN TRANSLATOR 3000 was stamped on each. *How convenient,* thought Lenora. She put one on.

"Hello," said Lenora. "How may I help you?"

CHAPTER NINE
Lenora Ascends the Summit

"Oh, thank heavens," said one of the penguins to Lenora. "We've been hoping a librarian would come by. You see, when the globe was built, we were dropped off in the wrong place. We're terribly lost."

"I think I can help you," said Lenora. "Climb aboard! By the way, what do you call a, er, *gathering* of penguins?"

"We're known as a colony, a rookery, or a waddle," said the birds, clambering over the side of the rowboat as it swayed wildly. "But really you can call us whatever you like. Unlike beluga whales, we're not hypersensitive about it."

When all the penguins were in, Lenora pushed away from the island. She was getting rather good with the oars. "I'll take you south," she said to her passengers, "though I can't stay long. I'm in a rush to ascend Mount Everest, but I've got to find the thing first."

"Oh, that's nothing," honked one of the penguins. "Penguins know all about the mountains of Earth. It's the first thing we learn in school." He waddled up to the prow and gestured with one wing. "Onward!"

Lenora heaved at the oars and the rowboat set off. Her rowing was definitely improving. Now her vessel surged through the waves as though its pilot had been born for the sea. Frozen tundra went by to starboard and she steered hard to the right, squeezing between Alaska and Russia and sliding over the floating letters of the BERING STRAIT. The air got warmer as she passed Japan, from which thousands of cherry blossoms blew into the sea, and near which a million jellyfish glowed in the waters. Navigating the many twisty passages of the South China Sea was tricky, but she managed.

And then she saw it. Off to the right, on the coast of Thailand:

KRUNGTHEPMAHANAKHON AMONRATTANAKO-SIN MAHINTHARAYUTTHAYA MAHADILOKPHOP NOP-PHARATRATCHATHANIBURIROM UDOMRATCHANI-WETMAHASATHAN AMONPHIMANAWATANSATHIT SAKKATHATTIYAWITSANUKAMPRASIT

The name of the city was so long they'd had to arrange the letters in a gigantic spiral. Krungthepmahanakhon Amonrattanakosin Mahintharayutthaya Mahadilokphop Noppharatratchathaniburirom Udomratchaniwetmahasathan Amonphimanawatansathit Sakkathattiyawitsanukamprasit was a much longer name than Llanfairpwllgwyngyllgogerychwyrndrobwllllantysiliogogogoch. Lenora had almost made a grave error. She got out her notebook and wrote down the longer name, then added: *Never make assumptions. Verify the facts.*

Soon they were back in the open ocean.

"There! There!" squawked the penguins, pointing north. And there was no missing it—across India and Nepal rose the tallest mountain around.

"Thank you," said Lenora with delight. She struck out south until they reached the shores of Antarctica. With all the rowing she'd been doing, she hardly felt the cold. "Will you be all right from here?"

"Oh yes, oh yes, thank you, librarian!" the penguins cried, flopping into the water with joy. "You have saved us! We name you our Honorary Queen!"

"Why, I'm so flattered," said Lenora, blushing. She shivered. "I'll visit again, in warmer clothes!" She rowed away as the penguins cheered.

She docked at India and set off for Mount Everest. When she reached it at last, it certainly looked like the highest point around—it would have required one Malachi standing on another's shoulders just to place a book upon the peak. But Lenora, who loved climbing trees or anything else she could find, thought nothing of clambering upward until she reached the very top. There, she stood on tiptoe, reaching up for a nearby railing that was rotating by, tantalizingly close—but she simply couldn't get hold of it. The tips of her fingers almost brushed the railing, but not quite.

She waited, but no other railings came anywhere near. Her plan had failed. Feeling defeated, she trudged back down the mountain and rowed south until she reached the penguins, who were happily doing belly slides on an icy shore. "I might be here awhile," she admitted to them. "I tried to get off the globe by climbing Mount Everest, the highest point on Earth, but I still couldn't reach high enough to get away."

"Oh, you never told us you wanted the highest point on Earth!" said a penguin. "Every penguin knows that's not Mount Everest at all. The highest point on Earth is Mount Chimborazo, in Ecuador."

"Oh!" said Lenora. "I never knew." She got out her notebook. *M. Everest not the highest point on Earth. Sometimes the thing everyone thinks is wrong.*

The penguin waved a flipper northwest. "It's

easy to find, too. The equator runs through Ecuador, which means Mount Chimborazo is exactly halfway between the north and south poles."

"Why, thank you!" said Lenora, and she wheeled about and set off for Mount Chimborazo. She felt a humming on her badge, and looking down she saw:

LENORA

— ⋄⋮⋄ —

SECOND ASSISTANT APPRENTICE LIBRARIAN

OFFICIAL COURT LIBRARIAN OF THE KINGDOM

OF STARPOINT SEVENTEEN

HONORARY QUEEN OF THE PENGUINS

Second Assistant Apprentice! Her heart swelled with a modest pride.

Soon she arrived on the coast of Ecuador. She gave her little rowboat a pat. "You're much nicer than that stupid balloon. Goodbye for now, dear rowboat."

Sad to abandon her trusty rowboat, but knowing she must do her job, she beached her vessel and headed for the highest mountain in sight. And sure enough, standing at the summit, stretching up on her tiptoes, she was just able to snag a railing. She grabbed on with both hands and gave an enormous pull. As she drew herself up, the library righted itself and she flipped onto her feet on the walkway. She had gotten off at a completely different place from where she had gotten on, and it took a bit of hunting and climbing up and down ladders and stairs until she found the Help Desk at last. And there was her patron waiting patiently. She went straight to him.

"I thought I had discovered the place with the longest name," she admitted, pointing to her notes, "in the fine and beautiful country of Wales. But then I found this much longer name in Thailand. I've got more research to do."

"Thailand?" exclaimed the patron. "Wait a moment . . . My true love always dreamed of learning to play *sepak takraw*—it's like volleyball but played with the feet—and it's quite popular in Thailand."

"That does seem like more than a coincidence," said Lenora, "but one should be careful with assumptions."

"No, I'm sure that's it!" said the young man, jamming his tricorne hat back onto his head and ignoring Lenora's warning. "Oh, thank you, librarian. Now I can send a letter to my true love!" And he rushed away.

A line of anxious questioners waited anxiously. Lenora grinned. "Next!"

CHAPTER TEN

Lenora Tackles the Unknown

Lenora had just finished helping two more patrons, the first a royal lady who desperately needed to know the only country that starts with Q, and the second a banker whose life depended on knowing the only country that ended with it (Lenora suggested the two discuss Qatar and Iraq over lunch together), when Malachi burst onto the scene looking rather disheveled, meaning a wisp of hair had escaped from her bun and her badge was ever so slightly askew.

"You are making excellent progress, Lenora," said Malachi. Beneath the Chief Answerer's cool demeanor, Lenora could detect a trace of urgency. "Fortunately for you, an even more challenging task has arisen. That is, if you are willing. You must decide right away."

Lenora's heart skipped at the prospect of an even greater challenge. But she knew she must not refuse.

She nodded firmly to Malachi, who led her away despite cries of protest from the long line of patrons. "No! We want her!" they shouted.

"Sorry!" Lenora cried out to them as she left, feeling terrible at abandoning so many needy patrons.

"For this task we must travel quite far," said Malachi. "Many miles, in fact. So it is time for you to receive a key to the Tubes." She held out a necklace upon which dangled a metal fob the size of a perfectly polished domino.

From the Chief Answerer's grave expression, Lenora could tell that great responsibility came with this object. Honored, she slipped it carefully over her head. She could feel the cold metal bouncing next to her badge as they walked.

Soon they came to an archway, above which had been carved the word TUBES. Inside the room beyond, several librarians waited in a line. When they saw Malachi they stepped aside and bowed. Several glass tubes bound with copper ran through the room in all directions. Each one had a door and a flight of steps leading up to it. Lenora remembered seeing tubes like this before—webs of them winding everywhere—outside the window when she had first entered the library.

Lenora felt the floor vibrate and then heard a *whoosh* as something shot through a tube and clunked to a sudden halt at the tube's door. It was a metal capsule, just large enough to hold one librarian, with several small windows and a door on the side. The door popped open and a librarian emerged.

Malachi gestured, and Lenora climbed in. Inside she found a single reclining seat with cracked leather upholstery. Surrounding the seat were thousands of small slots covering the walls, each one with a tiny metal tag above it. The tags said ANCIENT EGYPT and SHAKESPEARE and MODERN DANCE and everything else you could think of, including Lenora's former department of CALENDARS, for which she already felt a deep nostalgia. Then one tag caught her eye because it was illuminated brightly: UNKNOWN. Lenora had a feeling . . .

"As you may have guessed," Malachi said, reaching a long arm through the door (Lenora did not see how a giant like her could ever fit inside a capsule), "this is your destination." She placed a sharp finger on the illuminated tag. "The Tubes are pneumatic, which means they are powered by compressed air. Simply place your key in the slot for your destination, and you will be fired straight there. Try it."

Lenora slid her key into the slot for UNKNOWN. Instantly, the door to her capsule clanked shut. She heard a terrific *WHOOSH* and was squashed back hard into the soft leather seat. Her hands clenched the sides of her seat as she was pressed farther and farther back.

Gradually the pressure eased. She could feel she was going at incredible speed. She peered out through one of the windows, but everything was blurring by too fast to be seen until her capsule entered what seemed to be a giant cavern of ice. Her tube was hundreds of feet above the cavern floor, and far below her, Lenora could see librarians skating past with books in their arms. Then that view vanished, too.

She hoped the tube might whoosh outside for another terrific view, but sadly her seat soon swiveled in place so she was facing the other direction, and then the pressure came back and she was squashed again as the tube slowed. In moments, it came to a shuddering stop.

The door slid open. Lenora climbed out, feeling a bit dazed. She found herself in front of a large stone door, above which the words SECTION UNKNOWN were flashing in alarm. Standing next to the archway was Malachi.

Lenora gaped at the Chief Answerer. "How did you get here? Did you take another tube?"

"I have not used the Tubes in centuries," said Malachi. "I walked." She pushed open the door and they went inside.

The section, whatever it was, was about the size of Calenders, but unlike that section, it was a complete wreck. There were thousands and thousands of books strewn everywhere, tables and chairs upended, pens, paper, everything, in catastrophic disarray. Even heavy wooden desks had been overturned, their drawers open and the contents spilling out.

"What happened?" asked Lenora. It looked like a tornado had touched down here.

"A tornado touched down here," said Malachi. "We need to get it reorganized. But no one remembers what it was for. Your job is to reorganize this section and determine its purpose. We can't have unknown sections of the library; it's simply embarrassing."

"Of course," said Lenora, though she felt quite

intimidated. However would she organize all this? It looked as though it would take an army of librarians weeks just to put the books back on the shelves! But she had sworn to work hard, and work hard she would.

She turned to Malachi to ask how she had managed to walk many miles in only a few moments. But the Chief Answerer was gone.

Lenora sighed. Time to get started. Perhaps if she knew the subject matter for this section, she would be able to decide how to organize it. She went toward a pile of books and picked up a thick one from the top:

Orbital Mechanics for Total Morons

She didn't know what Orbital Mechanics was, but *orbit* sounded like it might have to do with outer space. She flipped through the pages and saw, as she'd guessed, loads of complicated math equations and pictures of spacecraft going around planets. Perhaps this section was for Space Travel? She picked up another book:

T is for Tardigrades

She couldn't even begin to guess what tardigrades were. She was about to open the book and find out when her attention was caught by a large box upon which had been stamped:

MOOSE

A moose in a box? That she had to see. She laid the tardigrades book back on the pile and opened the box.

She was rather disappointed to find not a moose but a battered suitcase on which had been stamped:

MOOSE: MANNED ORBITAL OPERATIONS SAFETY EQUIPMENT

And below this, in smaller red letters, was written:

Warning: Historical artifact for library exhibition purposes only! Do not attempt to leap from outer space in this MOOSE!

Well, thought Lenora, *I certainly won't be doing THAT.*

Curious to see what the MOOSE looked like, Lenora hefted the suitcase onto the Help Desk, which was of course just as messy as everything

else in the section. Someone had left some powdered doughnuts here. They had spilled across the
desk and there was powdered sugar everywhere.

Then Lenora noticed, standing just at the edge
of the powder, a red ant.

Lenora looked down at the ant.

The ant looked up at Lenora.

"Hello," said Lenora. "How may I help you?"

CHAPTER ELEVEN
Lenora Dodges Danger

The ant on the Help Desk began carefully plowing a path through the powdered sugar. Minutes later she had made what Lenora could see was the letter *H*. The ant stepped to the right and started anew. Eventually the *H* was followed by *E*, *L*, *L*, and *O*.

The ant looked at her expectantly.

"Oh," said Lenora. She took a tissue from an overturned box and carefully smoothed out the powder and the word *HELLO*. She also shook some powder from a doughnut to give the ant more space to write.

The ant began anew. *AN ACQUAINTANCE OF MINE NEEDS YOUR HELP QUITE URGENTLY.*

"Why can't your friend ask me themself?" said Lenora, and smoothed out the powder.

SHE IS VERY SMALL, the ant wrote. *AND SHE DOESN'T HAVE MUCH TIME.*

"If you think she's small," said Lenora, "then I imagine I would hardly be able to see her at all. Very clever of her to ask you for help. So what does she need?" She smoothed the powder.

THIS IS GOING TO TAKE FOREVER TO EXPLAIN, wrote the ant.

"Right," said Lenora. She thought about writing in her notebook that communication via powdered sugar was slow and laborious, but the point seemed rather obvious. "I think I'd better just ask your friend directly."

HOWEVER WILL YOU DO THAT? the ant wrote.

"We librarians have our ways," said Lenora, extending her finger to the ant. "Hop on."

The ant climbed on obligingly, and Lenora went to the tube. She scanned the tags until she found SHRINKING ROOM. After a short, high-pressure journey, they arrived.

"Wait here," said Lenora to the ant. "It's no good if you get shrunk, too." She walked in. Instantly the walls and ceilings seemed to vanish and she was standing on a perfectly flat plain that went on endlessly in all directions. Above her seemed to be nothing but open sky.

I've shrunk! thought Lenora, for even though she had expected this, it is still startling the first time one is shrunk to the size of an ant. She turned around and saw what appeared to be an enormous wall going straight up into the air. *That is the edge of the doorway,* she realized. It seemed miles away now. Nearby, she noticed a smooth bump in the floor. She walked over to it. It was a miniature tube. *Of course,* she thought. *Tiny librarians have to get around somehow.*

She got in and used her key to take the mini-tube back to the entrance, where she found the ant waiting patiently. Lenora was not at all startled to see that the ant was now at shoulder level. Close up, she was far hairier than Lenora would have expected, with jagged pincers and black, dead-looking eyes that reminded her of the Other Mother from one of her favorite books. She was glad that she and the ant had already established a friendship, for the sight of a human-size ant was, quite frankly, terrifying.

"I don't suppose that, like beluga whales, ants can mimic human speech?" said Lenora hopefully.

The ant shook her head, then turned and dashed away. Lenora raced to keep up, but the ant was *fast,* its six legs clattering along like perfect clockwork. Then the insect came to an instant halt. Just ahead of them, something enormous was descending from far above. It slammed down and the floor shook under Lenora's feet. She looked up and up and saw that it was a shoe the size of a battleship. Above the shoe, a leg stretched up like a skyscraper.

The shoe lifted up and away, and Lenora's gaze followed it.

The shoe was black leather, and above it was a dark pant cuff. Lenora felt instant dread, and she knew what she would see even before she looked higher—a black overcoat, and far above, what seemed like miles and miles and miles above, the brim of a black bowler hat.

Lenora realized with horror that, not having six legs with pinpoint maneuvering, she was certain to get squashed. Somewhere up there was the shoe, eager to slam back down on top of her. "Hey!" she panted, catching up to the ant. "You've got to give me a ride or something!"

The ant pondered, then lowered her head and clamped her pincers together. Feeling very brave, Lenora leapt onto the pincers, which made a rather more comfortable seat than you would think from looking at them.

The ant seemed to sense the danger, and she raced off in a zigzag pattern. The floor trembled as the shoe hit somewhere behind them. This mini-earthquake was no trouble for the nimble ant, however, and Lenora could see she was making a beeline (more of an antline, she thought) for an ant-size archway at the foot of an enormous wall.

In seconds, Lenora was ducking her head as they passed beneath the words ANT CITY, emblazoned above the arch. She slumped in relief, giving the ant a pat on her pincers. "Nice work!" she said. Looking back, she could see the tip of a shoe outside the entrance, and she grinned. "Foiled again," she whispered, because "foiled again" seemed like exactly the sort of thing she would expect one of the bowler hat people to say.

Just inside the entrance Lenora spotted a locker. On it was a label: ANT CITY COMMUNICATION KIT— LIBRARIANS ONLY!

Intrigued, she hopped from the ant's jaws. Entirely unsure of what she would find, she opened the locker by inserting her Tube key. Inside were several sets of what looked like earplugs. But from instructions printed on the inside of the door Lenora could see that they were meant to be inserted in the nostrils and were called Pheromone Interpreters. Lenora, naturally, slipped a pair into her nose.

Instantly, she was nearly overwhelmed by a blast of powerful scents coming from all directions. "Wow," said Lenora, looking at the ant, "is this how you talk to one another?" The ant did not move, but through the interpreters came a strong smell of something like honey, which seemed to indicate *Yes*.

Ant language—pheromones! Lenora scribbled in her notebook.

"Now then," Lenora said, hopping back onto the ant's waiting jaws. "What should I call you? I mean, what is your name?"

The reply came, not in words of course, but in a complex odor that smelled a little like lavender, a bit like fresh asphalt before it hardens, and a lot like cinnamon. "Cinnamon, I think I'll call you," said Lenora, "if that's all right with you."

Cinnamon produced a strawberry jam–ish scent that suggested to Lenora that she found this absolutely delightful, and off they went.

The sign advertising ANT CITY had not lied. She and Cinnamon were now hustling down the sunlit streets of a metropolis of ants, millions of them, in a maze of vast corridors, broad avenues, and ant superhighways arching through the air. Towering structures that seemed taller to Lenora than any skyscraper reached for the skies. Atop most of them, turbines spun busily. *Wind power,* thought Lenora. *Brilliant.* She also noticed that as ants passed one another, they touched their antennae together. *Ant handshakes?* she wrote in her notebook, to look up later.

They went over an arched bridge spanning a river, down which floated a structure that was composed of nothing but ants clinging to one another to form an island. Lenora was putting so many things in her notebook, she wished she had brought a spare. As she wrote, she pondered what it must be like to have millions of sisters (for Lenora knew that worker ants were all female) instead of being an only child.

At last they came into a round room with a

domed ceiling that had a hole at the top open to the blue sky. It made Lenora think of a class field trip to an observatory. In the middle of the room squatted the strangest animal Lenora had ever seen. It was about a quarter of the size of the ant and looked a little like a furless bear and a little like a caterpillar with eight legs. Each of its legs had a claw that the animal was working busily—one claw in a toolbox, one claw making markings on a chalkboard, two others playing chess (apparently with each other), another making a sandwich, and the final three making adjustments to a rickety, pointy vessel standing on three legs, its sharp tip aimed directly at the opening in the ceiling.

It was, undoubtedly, a spaceship.

CHAPTER TWELVE
Lenora Gets It

The spaceship was nothing like the sleek, solid vessels Lenora had seen before. The hull had been patched together out of various metals of all shapes and sizes. Windows bulged randomly in odd locations and, even more curiously for a spaceship, some of them were open. It looked like a house that had been put together in a hurry. A door on one side was just the size of the bearish, caterpillarish animal building the ship. Above the door were the words TARDIGRADE TRANSPORT.

The animal, which Lenora strongly suspected was a tardigrade, spotted her and promptly plunged a claw into the toolbox. After a bit of rummaging, she held out a headset to Lenora. "Let me guess," said Lenora. "It's a Tardigrade Translator 3000." She fitted it expertly onto her head.

"4000, actually," said the tardigrade. "Tardigrade speech is much more complex than that of, say, penguins. All they ever talk about is sliding around on the ice on their bellies, whereas we tardigrades have sophisticated conversations about interesting topics such as cryptobiosis and space travel."

"Space travel?" said Lenora. "I guess that explains the spaceship."

The tardigrade nodded. As she spoke she continued to move her claws about, simultaneously working on the spaceship, doing calculations, and playing chess with herself. Lenora felt certain that tardigrades would make excellent librarians. "You see," the tardigrade said, "yesterday my brother decided to voyage to the multiple-star system of Alpha Centauri, just over four light-years away, to start a new life. He invited me to go along, but I declined. I regretted the decision the moment I watched his spaceship take off. Thus I have built my own spaceship so I can join him."

"You built an entire spaceship in one day?" asked Lenora, amazed. But that would explain its appearance. Cinnamon, for her part, was scrambling all over the rickety vessel, emitting a fishy scent that suggested great curiosity.

"Oh yes," the tardigrade said. "I know it's not much to look at, but as it's made by experienced space travelers, tardigrade technology can be trusted utterly. I've even installed an artificial gravity generator, a technology humans have yet to discover. My only trouble is that my brother took all our books on how to get to Alpha Centauri. My first thought, of course, was to ask a librarian. I miss my brother terribly, and I fear I will never catch him if I don't leave soon."

Lenora's heart went out to what was clearly a very sad tardigrade. "Never fear. I can help you. I think. There was a book on orbital mechanics in my section. It seems to be the sort of thing you could use."

"Oh yes!" The tardigrade brightened. "Most certainly." She plunged a paw into her toolbox and handed Lenora a library card. "But not just that. I also need anything you can find about stops along the way, like the Oort cloud, and the Kuiper Belt, and the planets of Jupiter and Pluto—"

"They say Pluto's not a planet anymore," Lenora interrupted.

The tardigrade snarled. "As far as we tardigrades are concerned, Pluto is and always will be a planet. End of discussion."

Cinnamon, from the top of the spaceship, emitted a potent leather scent that indicated her complete agreement.

Lenora saw no reason to argue. She had always thought that Pluto seemed like a perfectly fine planet, whatever the adults might tell her. She took out her notebook. *Pluto is, always will be, a planet.* This she underlined firmly.

"I'll see what I can do," she told the tardigrade.

"But first—aren't you worried about such a long trip through space all by yourself? What if you forget you are in space and open a window?"

"Whyever would I worry about that?" sniffed the tardigrade. "We tardigrades are the hardiest survivors in all the animal kingdom! We are, in fact, the first animals ever to survive the open vacuum of outer space. We can survive one thousand times the radiation level of any other animal—"

Lenora began scribbling wildly in her notebook.

"—not to mention surviving being frozen to absolute zero! We can go decades without food or water. A mere trip to Alpha Centauri is nothing to a tardigrade. We are the ultimate survivors."

"Marvelous!" said Lenora. She wished she could do any of those things. One of the tardigrade's many talents might have helped her fix the horrific mess back in her unknown department. But the tardigrade needed her, and so she simply had to think of something.

"I'll be back as soon as I can," she said to the

tardigrade, trying to sound determined and confident. Cinnamon came racing down from the spaceship. Lenora patted the ant on her head. "Take me back to the Unshrinking Room, please." Cinnamon lowered her jaws obligingly.

As they wheeled away, Lenora's worries mounted. Her department was a complete wreck from the tornado. However would she find the books the tardigrade needed, assuming they were even in her department to begin with? It would take years of work for only one librarian.

They were back in the streets of Ant City now, surrounded by thousands of other ants streaming in all directions, carrying bits of food, or fleshy-looking things she supposed were eggs, and chunks of construction material . . . Thousands if not millions of ants, all in perfect order, feeding, building, their countless pheromone trails keeping them in constant coordination, acting as one to maintain their vast and lovely metropolis . . .

Lenora's gaze went up, up, up the tall towers that reached for the heavens, to the enormous wind turbines atop them, which she realized now could not only provide power, but maybe, maybe . . .

Lenora leapt to the ground and whirled to face Cinnamon. "I've got it!"

CHAPTER THIRTEEN
Lenora Leaps

Lenora paced back and forth along the street in Ant City, thinking out loud. "I'm going to need ants. Lots of ants. As many as we can get. Do you think some of the others would be willing to help?"

A scent like salty air came from Cinnamon in a way that suggested the ants would do anything to help a librarian.

"Thank you! Now, we don't have much time," said Lenora, "and we've got to get the message out as fast as possible." She pointed to one of the spinning turbines far above them. "I was thinking, maybe . . ."

Cinnamon understood immediately. Clasping Lenora ever so gently between her pincers, she raced straight up the side of the nearest tower. Up and up they went, Lenora thinking to herself that she shouldn't look down, then looking down anyway. Thousands of ants far below now looked like . . . well, ants. The wind up here was getting stronger, and now she could see more of Ant City, which stretched on to what seemed like infinity, a never-ending megalopolis, and she wondered if the world of ants dwarfed anything that humans had ever built or ever would build.

And now they had reached the turbine. Lenora managed not to think too hard about what would happen if Cinnamon lost her grip (which Lenora knew she wouldn't). The turbine's powerful blades cut through the air, the constant breeze up here keeping them in constant motion, a breeze which Lenora planned to employ to her own ends.

"Tell them the library needs their help!" called

Lenora, and Cinnamon, leaning out, sent her message into the winds, a message that smelled like plowed earth and burnt rubber and a basket of dried apples: *Librarian needs assistance!*

And the message worked, Lenora could see, when she and Cinnamon raced back down the tower, because dozens of ants had dropped everything and assembled below in long, orderly ranks. Soon Lenora found herself a general at the head of an army.

"Onward!" she ordered, and the columns marched rapidly through the streets and tunnels and out through the ANT CITY arch into the library proper.

"Watch out for anyone in an overcoat and bowler hat!" she called, pointing the way to the Unshrinking Room as the army hurried across the floor.

"Everybody in!" she cried, and her army rushed across the threshold.

In moments Lenora was back to her normal size. And the room was filling up with human-size ants.

They raced out into the corridor to make room as one after another unshrank. (Was it really unshrinking if they were small to begin with? Lenora decided to leave that question for another day.) Soon the ants were all rushing through the halls as startled patrons leapt out of the way.

"Sorry!" cried Lenora over and over. "Important library business!"

Traveling by ant was proving to be even faster than by Tube. In hardly any time at all, Lenora was back in her Unknown section. She installed herself near the desk and continued giving orders. Ants dashed around in all directions, stacking and shelving and organizing and straightening. They brought Lenora books and she told them where to put them. And it was exactly as she had suspected—with books on space travel and tardigrades and radiation and extreme cold, there was no doubt that she was in the Tardigrades section. She ran into the hallway and confirmed that TARDIGRADES now appeared above the entrance.

When everything was done and the Tardigrades

section was looking thoroughly professional and organized, Lenora asked the helpful ants to gather books on orbital mechanics and features of the solar system and beyond. "Oh, and bring the MOOSE, too," she told them. She never knew what might come in handy.

She climbed aboard Cinnamon for the journey back to the Shrinking Room. Lenora soon found herself standing in front of the tardigrade. "Will these do?" she asked, showing her the books.

"Oh yes!" said the tardigrade, clapping six claws together. "Precisely what I need. And just in time, as my spaceship is complete." The tardigrade gathered up all the books and clambered up into her ship. "Bon voyage! And do get some distance away, if you don't mind. When these rockets go off, it will get quite hot in here."

The ants hurried away. And then it hit Lenora:

The multiple star system of Alpha Centauri was more than four light-years away.

However would the library get those books back?

Lenora ran to the ship, up the ladder, and through the open door. There in the control room squatted the tardigrade in front of a control panel. Lenora's eyes widened as one of the tardigrade's claws pushed a button labeled LAUNCH.

The hatch behind her slammed shut and the floor shuddered and trembled. The words ARTIFICIAL GRAVITY ENABLED flashed on a computer screen.

"No!" shouted Lenora. But it was too late. Outside the windows, Lenora could see the dome's ceiling rushing past, then open sky. They were headed for outer space.

"Abort!" Lenora cried. "Abort!"

The tardigrade's eyes widened as it turned to face Lenora. "Sorry, but once I've launched there's no way back. You're just going to have to come with me to Alpha Centauri. Don't worry, you're more than welcome, and it will be a very exciting trip!"

Under different circumstances, Lenora would have been thrilled to join the voyage. She had always considered herself a potential space traveler, and she would so like to see the planet Pluto and its beautiful heart-shaped plain close up. But she dearly loved her job at the library . . . There simply had to be some way home.

Then she remembered—the MOOSE! She grabbed its suitcase. "What about this? It says something about leaping from outer space."

"My goodness," said the tardigrade. "Is that a MOOSE?" She waved some claws excitedly. "That might help. MOOSEs were made for astronauts in the 1960s in case they had to jump out of their spaceships and parachute to Earth."

"They could do that?"

"Of course!" said the tardigrade. "Probably. They only tested it off bridges, actually. But I'm sure it would have been fine." She opened the suitcase and removed the MOOSE, which looked something like a beanbag and nothing like anything you would want to jump from space in.

"I don't know," said Lenora dubiously.

"Never fear," said the tardigrade. "I can fix this

up so it will work perfectly. Once activated, you'll be surrounded by foam to cushion your landing, and this foldable heat shield will protect you during reentry. And in your shrunken state, you weigh so much less than a normal astronaut!" She grabbed a wrench and made several quick adjustments. "Now the rockets should direct you straight back to the library. Well?"

Lenora was torn. The box said clearly that the MOOSE was not to be used to jump from space. But the wise and experienced tardigrade had built a working spaceship in less than a day, after all. She looked out the window. They were now in space, and she could see the blue Earth below, and a glimpse of the stars she so longed to travel among . . .

"Best choose now," said the tardigrade. "If we fly much farther, you won't be able to get back by MOOSE."

With an ache of regret, Lenora gestured for the MOOSE. The tardigrade worked quickly, fastening straps and buckles until Lenora was blanketed, sleeping bag–like, with something hard against her back and a visor she could see through. The tardigrade waved goodbye, opened a door, and tossed her out into space.

The MOOSE spun end over end. First Lenora saw the long arc of the Earth's horizon, and all along the edge of its impossibly thin atmosphere—was there really so little air for such a big planet?—rippled shimmering puddles of yellows and greens, and she hardly had time to think, *The northern lights! Or possibly southern* . . . before she felt the rumble of rockets firing all around, positioning the heat shields behind her for descent. Her view swung away from Earth and she was looking straight out at a whole galaxy hanging there like pictures she had seen of the Milky Way . . . which she had never seen because she'd grown up in the city with bright lights that burned all night . . . but there was the Milky Way blazing across the cosmos like a silver river packed with floating gemstones, filling the void in their millions with all the colors that could ever be, the stars, the stars . . . Lenora reached out for them . . .

But then she was falling back into the atmosphere.

The sky faded to its normal blue just as the rockets switched off. Lenora, snug in the MOOSE, plunged back to Earth. Soon a parachute deployed, and she gently drifted to the ground. She allowed herself a last moment of heartsickness for what she had left behind, then found a handle and pulled. The MOOSE fell open, foam spilling everywhere. As Lenora stood, she felt a humming, and she looked down at her badge:

LENORA

———— ·⋮· ————

FIRST ASSISTANT APPRENTICE LIBRARIAN

OFFICIAL COURT LIBRARIAN OF THE KINGDOM OF STARPOINT

SEVENTEEN

HONORARY QUEEN OF THE PENGUINS

MOOSE PIONEER

She was in a tiny courtyard, surrounded by little columns. Far above, tall blades of grass, like skyscrapers to Lenora, waved in the gentle breeze. This seemed to be a miniature reading space for miniature readers, as books and comfortable chairs were scattered everywhere. And in front of her stood Malachi.

CHAPTER FOURTEEN
Lenora and the Enemy

"I t was the Tardigrade section!" declared Lenora, brushing off bits of stray foam. Quickly, she explained everything to Malachi about the spaceship and Cinnamon.

"Ah, of course," Malachi mused. "When I was a girl in Egypt, several tardigrades were among my most cherished playmates. They are very complex and interesting animals and entirely worthy of their own section of the library."

"Cinnamon must have already known that, or

she wouldn't have come to that section for help," Lenora said. "However did she know?"

"Oh, ants helped build many parts of the library, long ago," Malachi said. "They know it, perhaps, better than anyone."

Lenora could easily imagine that, considering the wonders of the vast ant metropolis. She resolved, if there were ever another Unknown section, to simply ask the nearest ant. "So what is my next assignment?" she asked.

"Hmm," replied Malachi, putting a finger alongside her sharp nose. "I don't think I'll give you one."

"What?!" Lenora exclaimed, feeling her heart plunge in her chest. "Is it because I forgot the books? I'm so sorry! I'll get them back. I'll build a spaceship. Here, let me go look up some plans." She turned to rush back to the Tardigrades section, where she was sure spaceship blueprints could be found.

"Don't be silly, Lenora," said Malachi. "It's not that at all. True, you made one mistake, but try to look at the big picture—you also reorganized a section in hours that would have otherwise taken months. Not to mention demonstrating the practicality of bailout reentry to Earth from space while you were at it. Don't let one minor setback throw you off track. No one is perfect."

Lenora disagreed. Malachi seemed perfect through and through. But she didn't argue. "Still— the books—it's my responsibility to get them back."

"Yes. So put in a request to have the librarians on Proxima Centauri b return them. I'm sure you can find the Transfers division yourself."

Everything did seem quite wrapped up. "Then why aren't you giving me another assignment?" She had thought of asking Malachi about the people in the bowler hats, then decided no, she wanted to solve her problems herself.

"You are a First Assistant Apprentice Librarian now, Lenora. It is time for you to choose your own assignments."

Joy enveloped Lenora.

She closed her eyes and breathed deeply. She could smell books, and even more, possibility. The choices were infinite. What did she want? From here, she could go anywhere.

When she opened her eyes, she was no longer in a tiny courtyard amid towering blades of grass, but standing on that grass, in a much larger courtyard. Malachi, also normal-size—if you could describe a ten-foot-tall Chief Answerer that way—was also standing there, and beginning to look a bit impatient.

Lenora did not bother to ask how they had unshrunk. With Malachi around, she was sure the Shrinking and Unshrinking Rooms weren't needed.

She heard a girl's cry: "Mommy! Hurry up!" Lenora turned to see a small girl with black pigtails and a smattering of freckles hauling on her mother's arm. The mother was gazing longingly down a hallway that was not in the direction her daughter was pulling. A sign with an arrow pointed down that hall:

NEW DIORAMA! BUBASTIS, ANCIENT EGYPTIAN CITY OF CATS!

There were some pamphlets next to the sign, and Lenora snatched one up as the mother tried to redirect the daughter. "Look, dear, a new diorama! Wouldn't you like to—"

"Mommy, come *on*!" the girl cried. "I have *so* many questions!" Dropping her mother's arm, she raced away down the opposite corridor. With a sigh, the mother hurried after her.

Lenora decided. "I would like to work wherever that girl is going," she said to Malachi, or would have said to Malachi, if Malachi were still there. Which she was not.

When Lenora had first come to the library, she was fazed by the Chief Answerer's sudden disappearances, but no longer. She ran after the mother and daughter. And as she went, she thought about the millions of stars in the Milky Way, gleaming against the void, and she wondered again about the words *Knowledge Is a Light*, and if they meant that knowledge was like the stars, seeming very close but actually far away, because you can't know everything (though she wondered about Malachi). But no, that didn't seem quite right somehow . . .

They came to a wide, steep stairway. On both sides there were ornate banisters, and Lenora was glad of these, because the height of the stairway looked rather uncomfortable. The freckled girl began to run up the stairs as fast as she could, leaving her distressed mother plodding behind. Lenora ran, too, thinking this energetic girl might need keeping an eye on.

The library fell away on both sides as the stairs went up and up. And up. And up some more. Lenora was beginning to wonder if the steps would ever lead anywhere, when at last they approached a majestic archway, above which HISTORY OF SCIENCE was chiseled in large, glorious letters.

The section was not particularly big, as Lenora had expected for such a grandiose topic. It was not that much bigger than Calendars, in fact. But while the section lacked in size, its books didn't. The suffering shelves groaned and sagged under the weight of the biggest books Lenora had ever seen. A few of them were sitting on wheeled carts, which Lenora imagined must be the only way you could move such heavy volumes.

There were other things, too, like a ceiling that was mostly a skylight through which the sun shone (leaving the whole section comfortably warm). And there was the Help Desk, which was covered in tools Lenora recognized, like rulers and compasses and microscopes, and tools she didn't recognize, like sextants and calipers and anemometers (she would look those up later). But there was little time to notice anything else, because the energetic girl was racing around the section in all directions, and patrons sitting at stone tables reading enormous books were casting annoyed glances in her direction.

Lenora went straight to the girl, hoping a book would be just the thing to calm her down. "Hello," she said. "How may I help you?"

"Oh, a librarian!" said the girl, stopping her

racing for just a moment. "I want the biggest book you have. I have *so* many questions!"

"*So* I've heard," said Lenora. "Why don't you sit still for just a moment while I find it?"

The small girl handed over her library card and plopped obediently onto a nearby chair, beaming with contentment, as Lenora hurried away, wanting to find that book before the girl darted off again.

Lenora did not have to search long. In the middle of the stacks was a pedestal, and on that pedestal stood a book that was taller than Lenora, and certainly thicker, too. It was a colossal specimen of a book. If only it could float, Lenora would have been able to sail the seven seas upon this tome.

It was a struggle to get it onto a cart. Lenora had to shove until the book toppled off the pedestal and onto the cart, and then push with all her might to wheel it back to the waiting girl. But the girl seemed pleased with this copy of *The Entire Scientific History of the Universe from the Planck*

Epoch to Now. Lenora wondered however the girl would take it with her, until the girl plucked it up with ease and danced away happily, waving it over her head.

Lenora sighed, wondering if this section required a rather larger and more muscular librarian. She sat in her place at the section's Help Desk and began to read the pamphlet about the new Bubastis diorama. But soon her reading was interrupted by something odd.

She was shivering just a little. She looked down at her arm and saw goose bumps.

She looked up at the skylight. She thought the sun would keep the room comfortable. But the sun didn't seem to be shining anymore. In fact, out of nowhere, dark clouds had gathered high in the sky.

That still didn't explain the cold, which was getting worse by the second. Patrons were beginning to look around with concern, muttering about the temperature.

Lenora thought perhaps she could find a thermostat

somewhere and turn up the heat. She peered beneath the desk.

And then she heard something.

A muffled crash, far away among the stacks.

And she thought:

Something fell.

Other than that crash, everything was quiet. The usual busy library sounds had gone dead silent.

In the midst of this heavy silence, Lenora heard a sharp rapping, like a cane tapping angrily on the floor. Coming closer.

She raised her head back above the desk—and there stood a man.

It was a man in a bowler hat.

CHAPTER FIFTEEN
Lenora and the Dark

"Hello," said Lenora, and she almost added *How may I help you?* But she knew the man in the bowler hat was not here for help. She had seen this one before—the one with the purplish, angry face and the too-tight overcoat, who had tried to keep the little boy out of the Astrophysics section before Lenora had become an official librarian. Her pulse quickened, and for an instant she wanted to bolt—but no, she would not let this man frighten her from her desk.

Instead she said quite calmly, proud to hear not the least tremor in her voice, "What do you want?"

The man scowled down at her from across the Help Desk. "I would like to make a complaint." His voice had a wet, heavy sound.

"This isn't the Complaints Desk," said Lenora shortly. "The Complaints Desk is down the stairs, across the hall, over the bridge, past the waterfall, then you take the fifth left after the third right and straight on 'til morning." Lenora had no idea if there was a Complaints Desk. "You'll also need ice skates."

The man chuckled nastily. He laid his walking stick across the Help Desk. The gesture felt too personal. Lenora barely stopped herself from brushing the cane off the desk and onto the floor.

"Oh, I don't wish to make a general complaint," he said. "My complaint is specific to you." He leaned forward, his thick, purplish fingers gripping the edge of the desk. Lenora pulled away in disgust. Everything about this man was odious, even the sweet scent wafting from him, which smelled like something that had been slathered on to mask some other, unpleasant odor.

Lenora was just about to respond when she heard another muffled crash, just like the first, coming from far away, back in the stacks somewhere. When she turned toward the sound, a second man in a bowler hat was standing there.

This second man carried a walking stick, just like the first, but other than that, they could not have looked more different. Rather than a purple puffy face, this man had smooth, fine features, and rather than being stuffed into an ill-fitting overcoat, his coat fit his slender frame perfectly. He beamed at Lenora with a most handsome, pleasant smile.

"At last we meet, my dear little Lenora," he said in what had to be the friendliest voice Lenora had ever heard. He fixed the first man with a scowl. "I must apologize for the actions of my associate here, as well as all of the others. Their hearts were in the right place, but they went about everything all wrong."

"Hmph," the first man huffed, folding his arms across his chest.

The second man turned his pleasant smile back to Lenora, but she did not return it.

"What do you mean, their hearts were in the right place?" she asked. "They tried to strand me in time and space, and trap me on a globe, and stomp me flat!"

"Yes, but they failed, didn't they?" the second man replied. "You proved to be much too resourceful and courageous for such crude methods. So no harm done."

"Uh," said Lenora, not sure how to respond. If you tried to harm someone and failed, it didn't mean no harm had been done.

"She's a threat," spat the first man. "I say we eat her now and get it over with."

Lenora didn't like the sound of that. Could she enlist any patrons for help? She felt she should not look away from the men, not for an instant, but glancing out of the corner of her eye, she could see the patrons strangely hunched and shivering in their chairs, oddly oblivious to the strange conversation going on amid the otherwise perfect silence. No help there.

The second man rolled his eyes. "No one is going to eat anyone. Lenora is an intelligent child. Once she understands how dangerous her actions have been, she's certain to cooperate."

"Dangerous?" asked Lenora in surprise. "All I've done is help patrons at the library! What's so dangerous about that?"

"We've seen the perfect example just now," the man replied. "In fact, we tried to stop you but couldn't get here in time. It's about the girl you gave that book to. It was a terrible, terrible thing to do, Lenora."

"It's only a scientific history of the universe," Lenora said. "What's terrible about that?"

The man sighed. "She is only a little girl, you see. A happy, contented little girl. But there are facts in that book that will . . . disturb her. Disrupt her. Cause her to feel fear, uncertainty, and doubt."

"Are the facts true?" Lenora asked.

The second man was about to answer when the first interrupted harshly. "Who knows? Scientists are wrong all the time! Scientists once thought the Earth was flat, until Christopher Columbus proved them wrong."

"That's not true at all," said Lenora. She had read a book about this very topic while sitting under a tree one day. The lengthy report she'd written about it had pleased her teacher. "Philosophers and scientists have known since ancient times that the Earth is round. A Greek scholar named Eratosthenes even calculated the distance around it more than two thousand years ago. And if Columbus hadn't ignored those measurements, he would have known he hadn't landed in Asia."

The second man laughed. "I told you," he said to the first. "Lenora is far too smart, and perceptive, and insightful"—here Lenora wondered whether the man thought showering her with praise would do anything but make her more suspicious—"for such foolishness. You can see why she makes such a dangerous librarian."

"I still don't understand the dangerous part," Lenora said. "The girl had questions. I helped her find answers. Maybe the answers will disturb her, but isn't it better for her to know the truth?"

The second man was continuing to smile his pleasant smile, but somehow Lenora felt it was just a little less pleasant than it had been before. "Even if you don't care about the girl's feelings—and with you being such a kind and charitable child, I find that surprising—you might consider the effect on the future. You see, that girl is going to read many more books after she finishes that one, and years from now, when she is grown, she is going to take the things she learned in those books and make new discoveries that will unsettle and disturb the entire world."

"Unsettle and disturb it how?" asked Lenora, feeling uncertain. For if—if—the man were telling the truth, it seemed that she was making a rather momentous decision.

"Billions will have their lives upended," the second man said calmly. "They will learn of things both very large, strange attractors that exist beyond the reach of today's telescopes, and things very small, powerful energies lurking beneath the capability of today's microscopes to see. Things more unexpected than you can imagine. Questions will be raised that will shock the world. Many will be frightened by this knowledge and will seek to retreat from it. There will be conflict."

That didn't sound good to Lenora at all. But at the time same, she felt that she was now on firmer ground. "I'm sorry there will be conflict and people will be frightened," she replied. "But that has happened before. Galileo unsettled people when he told them the Earth moves around the sun, and he was punished for it, and the new knowledge was banned, for a time. But aren't we glad we know the truth today?" She reflected on what an excellent book she had used for her report and resolved to see if she could find a copy in the library.

Now the second man's smile didn't seem pleasant at all but actually rather frosty. "Perhaps I misjudged you, Lenora," he said, and the frost was in his voice, too. "I thought you were wise enough to understand that children must be discouraged from asking questions that will make them curious and fretful. Perhaps I overestimated you. After all, you're just a child yourself."

"Maybe," said Lenora, with equal frost. "But I'm also a librarian. And I'm not going to hide the truth from anyone."

Now the second man's smile—frosty or pleasant or otherwise—was completely gone. "I am going to give you one last chance, little girl," he said. "One last chance before we turn back to the methods of my associate." In a swift gesture, the second man opened his coat—and though it was only open for an instant, Lenora glimpsed a deep darkness beneath it, like the view she had seen of outer space, but without the stars—and removed a sheet of paper. "I have here a list of books. Dangerous books. Books that will disturb young minds. Books you must remove from the library."

"I'll do no such thing," said Lenora, crossing her

arms on her chest. She could feel her heart pounding, but she kept herself steady.

The second man frowned toward the first. "It seems you were right," he said.

The first man grinned vilely and held out his hand. The second man took it.

Lenora recoiled as the two hands seemed to melt into each other, until there was just one long arm. But the arm was getting shorter, and then the two men were melting together like candles, and in moments there were not two men, but one man, twice the size of either, towering over Lenora with one huge bowler hat on his head.

The giant grinned down at Lenora with a mouth full of sharp teeth.

CHAPTER SIXTEEN
Lenora and the Light

Lenora broke for the exit. The giant man was partially blocking her, but if she ran she might make it—but then she realized guiltily that she had been on the verge of abandoning her patrons. She snatched up the nearest weapon she could find—a ruler—and raced out from behind the Help Desk. "Library emergency!" she cried, running from table to table and smacking the ruler against the tabletops. "Everyone evacuate this section immediately!" The hairs on the back of her neck stood straight, for she could feel the giant man lurking behind her, creeping closer as she ran about the tables. One by one, startled patrons came to life, suddenly noticing the giant man with very sharp teeth, and one by one they dropped everything and ran from the room.

As the last patron exited, the room darkened. Lenora looked up. The skylight no longer showed the light of day but instead showed an inky night with no stars, as though a heavy curtain had closed across the sky. Lights throughout the section flickered and went out. Everything was cloaked in darkness. Lenora could no longer see the exit. In fact, she could hardly see anything at all, because the only light left seemed to be a faint glow.

A glow that was somehow coming from Lenora herself.

She heard a rumbling growl to her left. She turned to face it, and her glow revealed the giant.

He was no longer a giant.

He was a monstrous thing, forty feet high, composed of pure darkness, black eyes glittering.

Shreds of his suit jacket flapped in tatters on each side, and within the tatters, within the darkness, Lenora could see images rushing past like broken bits of a movie—books piled up in flames, with people rushing to throw more books onto the fire, a hideous blaze with a horrid scent that stung Lenora's nose, and then there were wooden ships hurling fire at a tower on the edge of the ocean, a tower surrounded by walls of rubble, and then a great city full of domes where men on horseback fired arrows at fleeing people as buildings behind them burned and burned.

And through the streets just ahead of the archers raced a girl, a very tall, thin girl with a very sharp nose, her arms full of scrolls and her face full of terror.

Lenora thrust the ruler before her like a sword. "GET OUT OF MY LIBRARY!" she roared.

The thing rose over her and descended with a bellow, a whirlwind filled with screams. Lenora reared back to fight as the darkness enveloped her. She could no longer see anything, but she could hear shrieks filling her ears and she could feel hot tendrils snaking around her arm, and then—

The tendrils were torn away. Suddenly, there was brilliant, shining light everywhere, and she was surrounded by gentle warmth that covered her like a blanket. Outside the blanket, she sensed furious blows raining down, but the blows could not penetrate the warmth and could not harm her. The stench of burning books faded as light returned and Lenora could see the library again.

"Malachi!" Lenora cried.

"Yes, Lenora," replied the Chief Answerer, who had her arms around Lenora in a powerful embrace.

Above them the shrieking darkness, furious with rage, folded in on itself until it was nothing more than a dot. The dot vanished with a pop. Daylight returned to the sky.

Malachi released her and stood, staring hard at the spot where the darkness had vanished. The Chief Answerer was pale, and her hand was trembling ever so slightly, and for the first time Lenora realized that she herself was afraid, very afraid. Until just now, she'd been too busy to feel it.

"What was that?" she asked, when she had managed to recover her senses.

Malachi sagged onto the Help Desk, her shoulders slumped. Her hair had come loose from its bun and was down to her shoulders. The pencils in the bun were nowhere to be seen. She looked at Lenora with weary eyes. "Have you ever heard the term *Forces of Darkness*, Lenora?"

"Yes."

"Well," said Malachi, "it has been applied by many people to many things. But there is a true force of darkness, and that was it."

Lenora gazed at the spot where the darkness had vanished.

And then she knew.

"Knowledge Is a Light," she whispered.

"Yes," replied Malachi. "Knowledge Is a Light, Lenora. Throughout history that light has at times burned very dimly, and nearly even gone out, while in other times it has blazed up gloriously. Beings like the one you just met—they seek to extinguish that light."

"But whyever would anyone want that?" asked Lenora.

"The Forces of Darkness wish to control people, and it is ever knowledge that prevents them from doing so," said Malachi. "They can only rule where there is ignorance, they can only create fear where the truth has been hidden, they can only gain power when the light has been snuffed out. Librarians are their greatest enemy, and we have fought them throughout time, and always will fight them as long as that light burns anywhere, no matter how weakly. When I was a young girl very much like yourself, I vowed to dedicate my life to fighting the Forces of Darkness wherever I might find them. And so I have."

"And so shall I!" declared Lenora.

"It is a solemn vow, Lenora," said Malachi, "and not one to be taken lightly. Few have what it takes to fight this battle. But I believe you can do it."

Malachi rose to her feet, and she and Lenora

shook hands solemnly, Lenora on her tiptoes and the Chief Answerer bending down.

"I know we'll always win if you're there," said Lenora.

"I'm afraid that will not be the case," said Malachi gravely. "Sometimes we will win—as we did just now—and sometimes we will lose. I once fought them at a library in Alexandria and lost. And then again at a library in Baghdad, and I lost there, too."

Lenora remembered the tall, thin girl with her arms full of scrolls, running from the archers. "I think I saw you there."

"Yes," said Malachi. "But never fear—there have been victories as well."

There was silence as both of them pondered the many battles ahead. And Lenora remembered how, when the darkness had come, she glowed.

Finally, Lenora spoke. "Someday I want to be just like you."

Malachi smiled, a smile that was proud and perhaps sad, also. "If you put your mind to it, you will, Lenora. Someday. And congratulations," she said, pointing a sharp finger at Lenora's badge, "you are an assistant no longer."

For the badge now read:

LENORA

——◆—◦⋮◦—◆——

FOURTH APPRENTICE LIBRARIAN

OFFICIAL COURT LIBRARIAN OF THE KINGDOM OF STARPOINT

SEVENTEEN

HONORARY QUEEN OF THE PENGUINS

MOOSE PIONEER

MEMBER IN GOOD STANDING OF THE FORCES OF TRUTH AND

LIGHT, WHO HAS FACED THE FORCES OF LIES AND DARKNESS

AND PREVAILED

Lenora could not help but beam proudly.

"I must warn you," Malachi continued, "while it is very good to solve problems yourself, you should also not be afraid to ask for help if you need it."

Lenora flushed. "I should have told you about the people in bowler hats."

"Yes. Remember, Lenora, you are not alone in this fight, even if it will feel like that sometimes. You have allies, and you can rely on them to help you with the battles you are not yet ready to fight. Now, if I might ask a favor: Can you help out in Zoology? It's just next door. A pocket shark and a bonsai tree have a bet to settle."

CHAPTER SEVENTEEN

Lenora Leaps into Action

In the Zoology section, the pocket shark swam eager circles in its little tank while the bonsai tree looked on from its clay pot with breathless anticipation, or what passed for breathless anticipation, from something that neither looked nor breathed, exactly. Neither creature was much bigger than Lenora's outstretched hand, but they were both full of personality.

"Sharks," said Lenora, pointing to an open page in a book, "have been around for four hundred twenty million years. A very impressive number, I have to say."

The shark splashed its water proudly.

"Sorry," said Lenora to the bonsai. "But it says here"—she pointed to another large book open before her—"that Wattieza, the first tree, lived three hundred eighty-five million years ago." The bonsai wilted with disappointment. "Sharks are definitely older than trees."

The shark leapt from its tank, waving its fins in delight as the crestfallen bonsai's branches drooped.

"No one likes a sore winner!" Lenora admonished the shark, who wasn't listening. She sighed deeply, hoping the shark and the bonsai would both someday learn to take their losses and victories with more grace.

"Next!" Lenora called. She heard sniffling and tears. She looked around but didn't see anyone. Then she peered over the edge of the Help Desk. There she saw a very small boy in a very blue sweater with very sad tears streaming down his cheeks. "Oh my!" said Lenora, quite concerned. "How may I help you?"

The little boy looked up tearily. "I lost my kitten," he sniffed. "I had him in my arms and then he jumped out and ran away and his name is Mister Sparkles and—"

"Slow down, dear," said Lenora. "Whyever did you bring a kitten to the library?"

"He likes books about mice and I was gonna let him pick out his favorite and maybe some books about fish, too, and—"

"All right," interrupted Lenora. "A lost kitten is a serious matter, and we must begin the search right away. Never fear, however. We shall venture forth boldly and find Mister Sparkles."

Lenora took the boy by the hand. Encouraged by Lenora's confidence, he stopped crying. Together they searched up and down among the stacks. They looked high and low, then low and high, in front of and behind every shelf. They crawled underneath tables.

There was no sign whatsoever of Mister Sparkles, or any other stray kittens for that matter.

"Tuna," said Lenora.

"What?" sniffed the boy. He was ready to resume crying.

"If only we had tuna, we could lure him with the smell . . ." Lenora was thinking hard. Mister Sparkles seemed to have left the Zoology section, and from there he could have gone anywhere. Where would Mister Sparkles, or any cat really, go if they could go anywhere in the library?

She stood abruptly, nearly bonking her head on the table they'd been under. "Bubastis!" she announced.

"Bubastis!" cried the boy. "Of course! What's Bubastis?"

"An ancient Egyptian city," Lenora declared, "devoted to the worship of Bast, the goddess of cats. A whole city for worshipping cats, you know."

"I didn't know," marveled the little boy, his tears gone dry.

"The library has a diorama of Bubastis not far

away," said Lenora. "And I bet anything Mister Sparkles spotted it and absolutely had to go have a look. Wouldn't you, if you were a cat?"

The little boy nodded at this obvious truth.

Lenora pointed to some comfortable reading chairs with shelves nearby. "Our books on mice are over there. You pick out a few for Mister Sparkles. I'll be back soon."

And off she ran, out from Zoology and down the long staircase across from History of Science and down the hallway toward the diorama. (Actually, since no one was looking, she slid gloriously down the banister.)

Now something happened that had nothing to do with the search for the lost kitten, and though it did not seem important at the time, it would occupy Lenora's thoughts for a long time to come.

Her mind was completely on the kitten, and so she did not look twice when she passed a sign that said KENDO DEMONSTRATION. She did not even turn her head at the loud clackings and smashings that came from the room beyond. But then she heard a girl's high, sharp shout, a martial cry that seemed like it could shatter a brick wall. She simply had to see what was happening. She ground to a halt and whipped toward the sound.

The girl who had made the shout was standing stock-still over a fallen opponent. The girl seemed several inches taller and several years older than Lenora. Not much more could be told about her, because she was encased in armor. Her face was hidden behind a metal mask, and her armor was composed of a complicated system of black padding that protected every inch of her body. She was barefoot, and in her black-gloved hands she gripped a long sword made from bamboo slats tied with leather. Her opponent, who was struggling to his feet, was dressed just like her, and around them a large audience sat on the floor at a very respectful distance.

Lenora's gaze slid to the sign. Below KENDO DEMONSTRATION were the words JAPANESE SWORD-FIGHTING MARTIAL ART.

The girl's fallen opponent removed his mask

and climbed slowly to his feet as the audience broke into polite applause. But the armored girl did not move a muscle.

Sword-fighting! Lenora thought this looked like the most exciting thing she had ever seen, and that was saying something. She wanted to go closer and learn more—but then she shook herself. *The lost kitten!* How could she have forgotten, even for an instant?

Resolving to return to the kendo demonstration once Mister Sparkles had been found, Lenora tore her gaze away from the older girl and resumed her race to the diorama.

She knew when she was getting close because of the crowds, reminding her of the hordes that had come to see the new globe. People young and old were streaming past. There were school groups with their teachers and old ladies dressed like pharaohs. The crowd got rather thick, and Lenora found herself having to push.

Lenora thought there simply *had* to be a better way to get to the diorama. And there was. She spied a door in the wall marked LIBRARY STAFF ONLY. Beneath it was a lock that popped open easily when Lenora inserted her Tube key.

She found herself in a dim, rather dusty hallway. Running the diorama seemed to be an elaborate operation, for there were workers dashing everywhere, arms full of robes and headdresses and costumes, and there were people applying makeup to costumed actors who, Lenora supposed, performed in the diorama. She spotted an archway through which poured a velvety, dark blue light. Next to it was a chalkboard that read DIORAMA— PERFORMERS ONLY. Lenora was not a performer, but this was a lost-kitten emergency, and she knew it was time to break the rules. So she marched straight up to the archway—

"Wait!" a man called. Lenora turned. The man rushed over. His arms were full of makeup and costume supplies. "You can't go in there! Performers only!"

"This is a lost-kitten emergency," Lenora explained.

"Oh!" said the man gravely. "In that case, let me make you up in costume first. You can search for the kitten, and none of the spectators will be the wiser!"

"Thank you," said Lenora as the man ushered her to a nearby chair and looked her over appraisingly.

"I think you would make an excellent cat," he said after a few seconds. "It would be appropriate for the diorama, and who better to look for a lost kitten, eh?"

"Indeed," agreed Lenora, and the man went to work. He was very fast. She could feel him painting whiskers on her cheeks, and then he snatched something from a passing costume tray and attached it to her head, and Lenora could feel that they must be twitching ears. His hands flew around like birds, doing something around her eyes with makeup pencils and brushes, and when Lenora looked down she could see she had a furry body she didn't have before, and when she shifted uncomfortably in her chair she realized a tail had been added as well.

Really it all felt quite marvelous, and she had to fight back an urge to leap from the chair and begin exploring.

"There!" cried the man, stepping back. "Some of my finest work, if I don't mind saying so! Now go find that kitten!"

"Yes!" cried Lenora, and she leapt from the chair. To her surprise she bounded several feet into the air and landed as lightly and easily as could be. Ahead of her were concrete steps, and she practically flew up them to the top, hardly noticing that she was doing it on all fours. There was an open door, and beyond it:

CHAPTER EIGHTEEN
Lenora Races Across the Sands

Sand, red sand, on and on to a dark blue horizon. Above that was what appeared to be a perfect night sky, black as stone, twinkling with fiery stars next to a sliver of moon. Lenora supposed those must be lights in the ceiling. The library really had done a terrific job on the diorama.

To her right, she could see the edge of the sand and then a velvet rope and, beyond that, crowds of people lining the library hallway, all of them pointing at various details and either gawking in awe or taking notes.

To her left, Lenora saw nothing but ancient Egypt, stretching over the starlit sands. That dark blue horizon had to end in a wall, cleverly concealed by expert designers, but you wouldn't know it from looking.

Speaking of looking, there was something astonishing about her vision: There was *more* of everything. She could see much farther to the left and the right than she normally could. She supposed it must be from what the makeup artist did with her eyes. She wanted to write it down in her notebook, but she had left it behind. And besides, when she looked down at her hands—which looked not like hands but more like paws now that the makeup artist was done with them—Lenora thought she could probably not hold a pencil right now anyway.

She also realized at last that she was on all fours, as though that were the most natural thing in the world. It was so natural that she couldn't imagine why she had ever tried to stand on two feet. That seemed so unbalanced and awkward—however did one keep from falling over? And the smells! They were coming from everywhere and calling for her attention. She bent her nose low to the sand and sniffed. Yes, rather faint, but she was *sure* it was another cat. And then she spied tracks—kitten paw prints—chasing away across the red desert.

Lenora bolted, following the tracks, bounding on all fours at terrific speed. As she ran, she wondered how she could spy these prints so easily in such dark surroundings, but it wasn't just those— it was everything. She could see almost as well in the semidarkness as she normally could during the day. The only trouble was that faraway things—like those three pyramids in the far, far distance—were very blurry. Lenora had never been nearsighted before, but she supposed this was what it was like.

She hardly had time to wonder about it before her attention was snatched by a burst of motion at the edge of her vision—a mouse! She burned with desire to chase it—only to play, of course—but she had a job to do. Firmly, she fixed her attention on the kitten tracks and continued her dash through the desert night.

"Mommy, look, a cat!" she heard a child cry, and she was very glad for the makeup. If she had been her normal self, it would have ruined the illusion.

She galloped up one side of a towering dune, warm sand whisking away from beneath her paws. As she crested the dune she skidded to a halt, transfixed by the sight below her.

It was the Temple of Bubastis. It had to be. She knew it in her heart of hearts. Also, there was a huge sign in front of it that said TEMPLE OF BUBAS-TIS. There was a high stone wall around the temple, and around the wall flowed two canals filled with dark water reflecting the twinkling lights above. The flowing waters ended at an entrance in front. Trees lined the banks of the canals. Sculptures were everywhere, mostly of cats, with the largest one being a huge statue of a woman with the head of a cat. The plaque beneath her read:

And below that it read: TRANSLATION FROM HIEROGLYPHS: BAST—GODDESS OF CATS.

To either side of the statue of Bast stood a fierce-looking man and woman—performers—holding sharp spears and looking protective. Beyond that was the edge of the diorama and a murmuring crowd taking pictures and pointing.

Something moved, capturing Lenora's attention instantly. The movement was at the very top of the red stone temple. She only saw it for a moment, but she knew what it was. She flew down the side of the dune to the entrance. The guards moved to block her way, then they noticed her badge (it was still affixed to her fur) and moved aside with smiles. Lenora nodded to them and ran inside the wall.

There seemed to be no way into the temple itself. No doors, just soaring columns and alcoves in which there were more huge statues grinning or scowling or gazing thoughtfully at little, furry Lenora far below. Lenora eyed the sides of the temple. They were very, very steep, but not completely straight up.

She got a running start.

When she leapt onto the side of the temple, claws popped out from within her paws. She felt them strike the red stone and grip hard. She ran harder than she ever had in her life, digging in with those claws, up the steep incline, her tail waving to keep her in perfect balance. Just when she thought she might tip over and fall, she reached the roof.

Cool winds blew gently past, bringing dry, sandy scents. The stars seemed quite close now, and when Lenora looked behind and down, the man and woman guarding the entrance looked tiny. Beyond them stretched the enormous crowd, its murmurs somehow still audible. (*Why is my hearing so much better?* she wondered.)

Ahead of her, squatting on the very edge of the roof, sat the kitten, tail twitching.

Lenora padded over and sat beside him. *It would be a very long fall from here,* she thought, and yet she felt not the slightest fear.

"Hello," she said to Mister Sparkles, or rather she meant to say. But what came out was "Mew!"

The kitten looked at her and blinked slowly. Lenora felt she had never seen a friendlier gesture, and she blinked slowly back.

"Mew mew mew!" said the kitten, which Lenora understood to mean "Look at them! Look at all my worshippers."

"Mew . . . ," said Lenora, with hesitation. She didn't want to disappoint Mister Sparkles, but she had to suggest that the spectators were here for the diorama, not to worship cats (though at this moment that seemed a most logical thing to do).

"Mewmewmew?" the kitten replied, and Lenora could see he was still disappointed, despite her efforts.

"Mew!" said Lenora cheerily, asking the kitten if it wasn't better to be loved than worshipped anyway, and didn't the little boy in the blue sweater love and miss his kitten so much?

Mister Sparkles pondered this, and Lenora could see that as he thought of the boy, his eyes brightened. "MEW!" he cried piercingly. "MEW!" And in those mews, Lenora could tell the kitten loved and missed the boy so terribly much, too.

Together, she and the kitten ran. They scampered down the steep wall. They romped across the desert, batting playfully at each other. Soon they were at the edge of the diorama, where Mister Sparkles assured Lenora he would run straight to the boy in the blue sweater. The kitten and Lenora nuzzled their noses together before they parted.

Wearily, Lenora went to have her makeup removed. She wasn't used to running everywhere on all fours and was getting a little sore. When she was back in normal clothes, she returned to the dim, rather dusty hallway. She had to hurry back to Zoology, which she'd left unattended. Just as she reached for the door, she felt a humming on her badge:

LENORA

— ·:· —

THIRD APPRENTICE LIBRARIAN

OFFICIAL COURT LIBRARIAN OF THE KINGDOM OF STARPOINT

SEVENTEEN

HONORARY QUEEN OF THE PENGUINS

MOOSE PIONEER

MEMBER IN GOOD STANDING OF THE FORCES OF TRUTH AND

LIGHT, WHO HAS FACED THE FORCES OF LIES AND DARKNESS

AND PREVAILED

LOST KITTEN PATROL

She admired her badge but also felt bashful about the long list of titles. It was beginning to seem too much like bragging. Perhaps she would ask Malachi for a badge more like the Chief Answerer's, with words that were simple but summed up everything, something like—

She did not finish the thought, for a trapdoor opened beneath her feet, and she fell through the floor.

CHAPTER NINETEEN
Lenora Falls into a Trap

Lenora fell in total darkness, wishing desperately that she had her agile cat body back as the wind whistled past her face. She didn't have time to think much else before she landed on a pile of something soft.

She had never been in such perfect, inky darkness before. She sat up and felt around herself to see what she had landed on. It felt like a bunch of pillows. Her hand found something small and rectangular. She picked it up, and it rattled in her hands.

Turning it over, she realized it was a box, and the middle section could be slid open. She felt inside and discovered it was a box of matches.

She struck one.

She was indeed sitting on a pile of pillows. Beside the pile was a lantern, and beside that was a piece of paper. She looked at the lantern, thinking that she had never used one before, when the heat from the match flame began to burn her fingers. She blew it out and all was darkness once again. She crawled toward the lantern until she could feel it with her hand, then lit another match. This time she looked at the paper. On it was written: *Lenora— unscrew lid and light wick.*

So all this was meant for her. This was somewhat alarming. Was it a trap? But she reasoned that if anyone—for example, someone in a bowler hat—were trying to harm her, there wouldn't have been any pillows. So she lit another match, unscrewed the lantern's lid, and touched flame to wick.

Now there was considerably more light. She put

the lantern's lid back on and stood, taking the light up by its handle, to have a look around.

She was standing in an old, musty stone vault. It looked a bit like a reading room from the library. But here, everything was covered in thick dust, and the bookshelves casting flickering shadows in the lamplight were all utterly barren. There was a Help Desk, but it was unoccupied. The only interruption in the heavy dust was a set of footprints, from bare feet. They entered the vault from an archway at one end, circled the pillows a few times, then left the way they had come. Besides this barefoot person, it seemed no one else had been in this part of the library for a long, long time.

It was quite obvious to Lenora that the footprints belonged to whoever had left her a safe landing spot and equipment to see by, and so must be a friend. Lacking anything better to do, she stepped off the pillows and followed the trail, her lantern casting weird shadows and her shoes kicking up puffs of dust. Her footsteps, echoing around the walls, were the only sound to be heard.

Past the archway, she entered a dusty, deserted hallway. On either side were open doorways. It seemed that these ought to lead into different sections of the library, and indeed, they had signs above their doors. But the signs were blank, and inside the rooms, the shelves were empty.

Lenora noticed it was getting darker and looked at her lantern. The wick was lower than it had been before. But there was a lever on the side of the lantern, and turning it raised the wick. Everything was brighter now, but she could not help but wonder how much wick and fuel she had. She did not want to be trapped in this place in complete darkness.

She looked for the footprint trail and realized it was gone. She turned around and could not see it. How was that possible? The hallway was nothing but a straight line. But somehow, the footprints had vanished.

There was nothing to do but hurry forward.

Section after section passed by, none of them with names. Then Lenora stopped. She'd come to the first doorway with words chiseled above it: MINOAN LITERATURE.

Despite her desire to escape, Lenora couldn't help herself. She peeped inside.

These shelves were not empty but filled with row after row of clay tablets. She walked along, peering at them. They were covered in writing that she could not decipher.

You are not the only one, Lenora, said a quiet voice near her shoulder. *No one can read them.*

Normally when one thinks one is alone in a dark, possibly underground vault, one is startled out of their wits when a voice suddenly speaks out of nowhere. But this voice, a girl's, was so soft and friendly and had such a charming accent (which Lenora could not place) that Lenora was instantly at ease. At ease, despite the fact that when Lenora turned around, no one was there.

"Hello?" said Lenora breathlessly.

Hello, said the unseen girl. She seemed to be speaking from right next to Lenora.

"Are you a ghost?" asked Lenora with excitement.

She'd never believed in ghosts, but how lovely if they did exist, after all!

No, came the reply, and there was sadness in the word. *I'm not a ghost. I'm a memory.*

"Whose memory are you?" asked Lenora. A reasonable question.

No one's. I'm a lost memory. Lost, like the words on these tablets, which were made on the isle of Crete thousands of years ago.

"But can't they be translated?" said Lenora. "Egyptian writing is thousands of years old, but we can translate that."

This is a language called Linear A. And it has never been translated, and may never be. We know little about the Minoans, who once had a great civilization, because of this.

Lost languages. Lenora had never thought about this. "I suppose many old languages must have been lost."

Not just old ones, said the girl. *Languages that are spoken even today are being lost, bit by bit. There are people trying to save them, but it is very hard.*

And then it struck Lenora. The vault, these empty rooms . . . "This is lost knowledge," she whispered in horror. "All these rooms should be filled with the things we've lost."

Yes, said the girl. *Lost, like me.*

"Who are you?" asked Lenora. Now she was spooked. Not by the girl, but by the vast amount of empty space and what it all meant.

I'm a librarian, said the girl. *Or at least, I was, a thousand years ago. I'm still sort of a librarian, here, though there isn't much to do.*

Lenora thought her heart might break wide open.

The girl continued. *I lived in a small village in Japan, long, long ago. It was a poor place, but it was on an important road, and many travelers passed through. Some of them left behind manuscripts and scrolls, forgotten in their haste to move on to more important places. I could not read them, of course, but I thought they were beautiful, especially the ones with pictures. So I began to collect them.*

Sometimes a traveler would read some to me, and by paying careful attention, I taught myself to read. And I discovered that travelers were speaking of my collection to one another, and soon new arrivals were asking to see it. Some of them asked me if they could buy some of the manuscripts, and in this way I learned they were valuable. But I did not collect them so that I could make money. Instead I would trade a manuscript for which I had two copies for a manuscript that I lacked. In this way, I eventually had a library of no small size.

"That is wonderful," breathed Lenora. How she wished she could visit this girl and her library, one thousand years ago.

Yes, said the girl, and her voice took on a wistful tone. *But it was not to last. One night, a stranger came to our town. He wore a black kimono, and he asked to see my library. Unlike others who asked, he did not seem delighted at the sight but quite angry. And that night, the small building housing my library burned to the ground. All was lost. And I soon heard that a new road was being constructed, one that would take travelers around our town. I was never able to rebuild my library.*

"A man in a black kimono," said Lenora. "Was he . . ."

Yes, said the girl. *The Forces of Darkness. You can always tell when it's them. They go after the libraries.*

Lenora was silent for a few moments, thinking of this. Then she realized that the girl did not seem at all surprised by her presence in this forgotten section of the library. "Do you know why I'm here?" she asked. "Do you know who dropped me through the trapdoor and left the pillows and lantern?"

Yes, Lenora. I do. But I can't tell you. Please— she said this because Lenora had already opened her mouth—*don't ask anything more. You'll understand soon. Now follow me. There are several things I must show you.*

Lenora bit her lip and nodded. She wondered how she would follow someone who was invisible, but the girl continued to talk, and as the voice moved along Lenora found it easy to follow. They left Minoan Literature and returned to the central hall, continuing along the way Lenora had already been going. As they walked, the girl pointed out rooms containing the complete works of the poet Sappho, and the lost plays of Sophocles and Shakespeare, and a translation of the Voynich manuscript. Lenora tried flipping through the pages of some of these, but they were all blank.

"I don't understand," said Lenora. "How can all these things be here if they have been lost?"

Because we know they exist, and they may yet be found, replied the girl. *For example, we find new scraps of Sappho's poems now and then. When this happens, we move them up to the library—from the darkness into the light.*

"And the rooms that are simply empty," guessed Lenora, "that's the knowledge we've lost and don't even know it."

Yes, said the girl. *Like my library, and even my town, which was destroyed in a tsunami decades after I died. Nothing was ever written down about any of it, and so it's all forever lost. Forever forgotten. Just like me.*

"We should write more things down," said Lenora quietly.

The girl did not reply. There was no need.

We're here, she said a moment later.

Lenora did not need to be told what to do next. Jutting out from the wall was a tube the size of her arm, flared at one end. She'd seen these before at playgrounds—listening tubes that let you hear what someone rather far away is saying at the other end. Trembling without quite knowing why, Lenora put her ear to the tube.

Voices. A man was talking, somewhere in a room far away, but the listening tube brought his words to Lenora as though she were beside him.

It was also especially easy to understand the man, because he had an extremely loud, booming voice. "To be honest," he was saying, "you've got a great, great library here. The biggest, most beautiful library. And no one is saying you haven't done a fantastic job with the place. I mean, they are saying that, but you know, that's so, so unfair."

A woman's voice then spoke up; Lenora recognized it immediately as Malachi's. But she could not tell what the Chief Answerer was saying, because the loud man kept talking as though Malachi hadn't said a word.

"And I think you'll be just as excited as everyone else about the new leadership on the Board, and the exciting changes we've got coming, with a new vision for the library's mission—"

Malachi did not sound excited from what Lenora could hear. She was still trying to interject, but the man simply wouldn't stop talking.

"—for example, the question of profitability. The library simply isn't making money."

And here the man paused for breath long enough for Malachi to say, "The value of a library cannot be counted in money."

The man continued as though Malachi had not spoken. "And the new leadership thinks we could do better, by running it more like a business. Your role will continue to be very important—extremely important of course, almost no one would say otherwise. There will be a lot to do, getting rid of the less profitable books and moving in new ones, and loyal team players like yourself will be critical to the new process—"

Malachi broke in again, this time quite angrily, Lenora thought. The man was saying awful, untrue things—and what was this about the Board? Lenora had never heard of the Board. The two voices continued to talk over each other, the man continuing as though Malachi was not speaking, and Malachi persisting nevertheless.

Lenora! the Japanese librarian said, urgency in her voice. *You must go!*

Lenora pulled herself away from the listening tube reluctantly. She wanted to hear the rest of the conversation. "Why?" she asked.

Because, said the girl, *they're coming.*

CHAPTER TWENTY
Lenora Goes

Lenora did not need to ask the Japanese librarian who was coming.

Look down to the far end of this hallway, the girl said. *Do you see it?*

In the distance, a soft glow. "Yes," said Lenora.

Follow it, said the girl. *Hurry. Do not turn back.*

"What about you?" asked Lenora anxiously. "Will you be all right?"

No reply came. Lenora waited a few moments, then hurried toward the faraway glow. *You are not forgotten,* she thought as she went. *I will remember you.*

Lenora ran, kicking up a tremendous cloud of dust as she flew past room after room of lost knowledge. The glow at the end of the hallway grew larger, and soon Lenora could see that it came from another lantern, just like hers. And holding the lantern was the tall, sword-fighting girl from the kendo demonstration. She was still wearing her black padded armor, and her face was still covered by the metal mask.

"Who are you?" asked Lenora.

"I'm . . . a friend," said the older girl, her voice muffled by the mask. "Here, take this." She held out her lantern. "Yours is about to run out of fuel."

The girl seemed so commanding and decisive that Lenora took the new lantern without thinking. And just as the girl had said, Lenora's old lantern sputtered and went out moments later. She sat it on the floor, and as she did she noticed again the tall girl's bare feet. "If you're a friend," Lenora asked, "why did you drop me through a trapdoor?"

"I didn't," replied the girl. "It was a trap, set for you by the Forces of Darkness. Fortunately, I was a few steps ahead of them. This time." She pointed toward the last door in the hallway, an archway above which some letters were bolted.

Lenora read them aloud. "The Labyrinth of King Minos of rete."

"Crete," said the girl. "The *C* fell off. You'll have to find your way to the center."

"Won't you come with me?" asked Lenora. It was rather dark in there, and now there was only the one lantern.

"I can't," said the girl.

"Why not?"

"Because," answered the girl, "they're coming." With that, she raised her sword, and this time it was not one made of bamboo slats but cold, glistening steel, blazing in the lantern's light.

Lenora turned in a circle, holding the lantern

high. She didn't see anyone coming. But now she could see that the hallway ended in an old stone wall, and that wall had four newer-looking metal doors in it. The doors began to slide open.

A robot emerged through each. These robots looked like spindly metal broomsticks on wheels, with two arms jutting out. At the ends of the arms were not hands but sharp swords. Worst of all were the bowler hats atop each robot's head.

The robots advanced as Lenora greatly wished for a sword of her own.

The girl did not hesitate but flew to the attack. Lenora's breath caught at the girl's incredible speed as she dashed forward with balletic grace. With a high, sharp shout and a strike so swift that Lenora hardly saw it, her sword slashed and a robot was cut in two, its arms and bowler hat tumbling across the dusty floor.

The three remaining robots bore down on the girl, their six swords flashing as they struck at her again and again. Somehow she was managing to block them, backing up as the robots advanced.

"Hurry!" she cried to Lenora, pointing at the arch into the labyrinth of King Minos of [C]rete.

Lenora fled through the arch, then stopped. Should she leave the girl alone? But what could Lenora do against robots with swords? She turned around anyway.

The armored girl had her back against a wall now as she fought. She seemed to know what Lenora was thinking, because she called out, "You must leave me, Lenora. Never fear, your friends are here to help you." Then the girl gestured, and a solid metal gate crashed down across the archway, cutting Lenora off from the battle.

From the other side of the gate, Lenora could hear the crash and whir of a terrific fight. Lenora wondered how the girl could possibly combat the robots now, for without the lantern, she must be in complete darkness. But there was nothing to be done.

Lenora turned. Lantern light filled a long stone hallway. Corridors branched off in all directions. *Take every right-hand turn,* she thought. Placing her right hand on the wall, she ran forward, taking every right turn, never lifting her hand from the wall. Soon she came to a door above which was written the word CENTER. And there beyond it, her lantern light glinted off—

"Bendigeidfran!" Lenora cried joyfully, racing forward. "We have to go back and help that girl!"

The friendly robot's eyes glittered a happy green. "Don't worry about her, Lenora," he said. "By the way, I did find my chip. It was buried in the sands in front of the Sphinx, just like you said! Now, keep moving forward and do not be afraid. Your friends are all around you." He had a kind of wand in his hand, which he pointed at the floor and moved in a circle. A hole appeared, just large enough for Lenora, and from it burst a strong scent of ancient decay. "This way, quickly! I'll lower you down."

With her lantern in one hand and Bendigeidfran's strong hands gripping the other, Lenora was lowered into . . . whatever it was. "What is this?" she asked the robot as her feet touched a dirt floor.

"Oh, it's just the tomb of Genghis Khan," said the robot. Lenora looked up in alarm, but Bendigeidfran was gone.

A tomb? Lenora shivered and wished she'd known that before she got herself lowered into it. Not that she had much of a choice, but she would have liked to have been prepared. She swung the lantern around and noted there was very little in the spacious tomb, which was lined with walls of dirt, besides a coffin—she left that alone—and strangely enough, what appeared to be the skeletons of six cats. She could not stop herself. *G. Khan, tomb, cats. Why?* she scribbled in her notebook. Then she wondered what to do next, for there appeared to be no way out of the tomb. For the moment, she was trapped.

And then she heard a *thud*. And another. On the third *thud,* earth burst from one wall of the tomb, and through it charged another of the bowler hat robots. It raised its flashing swords and charged at Lenora.

CHAPTER TWENTY-ONE

Lenora Leaves

Trapped in Genghis Khan's tomb with a killer robot, Lenora had nowhere to run.

The robot churned forward, and she saw that this one did not have wheels but treads like a tractor that made it perfectly suited for the dirt floor.

She looked wildly around, wishing that whoever had buried Genghis Khan had thought to leave a few weapons lying around, or maybe a shovel to dig a hole through the wall, or—

And then she saw that something *was* digging

a hole through the wall opposite the charging robot. The dirt wall crumbled, then fell away in chunks, and suddenly there was a hole just Lenora's size, with millions of ants pouring out, all of them rushing straight toward the robot, which turned on its treads and fled the way it had come. But it was not fast enough, for the industrious ants had it buried up to its neck before it could make a getaway.

On the wall, a few hundred ants assembled to form a message, and the message said:

GO LENORA GO

"Thank you! Thank you!" Lenora cried to her friends the ants, sure that Cinnamon was somewhere among them. Through the hole she went, until she came out into a natural cave, stalactites coming down from the ceiling and stalagmites coming up from the floor. Its floor was sheer ice, and the ice reflected a natural light, for the cavern's ceiling was glowing with phosphorescent somethings.

But Lenora had no time to wonder about that,

for weaving toward her were three robots with bowler hats, swords high. Instead of wheels or treads they had ice skates.

Lenora tried to run, but she was on ice now, no skates at all, and she slipped and fell, her lantern spinning away. She was trying to get to her feet when something black sped past. First one, then another, and now she could see they were a whole colony of penguins, waving their flippers as they slid by on their bellies. One of them snatched up the lantern with its beak. Lenora threw herself forward on her belly, too, and she was caught up amid the colony of black-and-white birds, carrying her along like a boat in a river. The slope got steeper and the colony got faster, and the robots on their skates were long gone by the time the penguins and Lenora hit full speed.

She wanted to slide on like this forever, but she knew she could not, and soon the colony spun her and the lantern down a side passage away from them. Lenora called out, "Thank you, my friends!" and the penguins squeaked and honked their goodbyes. (*That much* she could tell without a penguin translator.)

The steep slopes ended and Lenora came to a sliding halt. She grabbed the lantern and stood.

She was in another abandoned reading room. This one had only one small arch leading out. In front of it stood the armored girl.

There was no question she'd been in a battle. Her black padded armor was ripped and torn. The metal mask was dented. And she was breathing hard, but she was standing tall, sword at her side.

Lenora went to the girl. Lenora was full of questions, and she opened her mouth to ask one—

"Sorry," said the girl. "No time left. Bendigeidfran brought me here, and he's got to get me back." She went to one knee, so that she was the same height as Lenora. She held something out and dropped it into Lenora's hand. "When the time comes, you will need this. Don't worry, you'll know."

Lenora looked at the thing she'd been given. It was a pure white card. On one side was a magnetic strip. She turned it over, and on the other side she saw the words LIBRARY CARD in glittering letters, flashing all the colors of the rainbow. The card seemed to hum with inner power, causing her hand to tingle.

"But who are you?" Lenora cried.

"No time," said the girl, and she gave Lenora a push, sending her stumbling toward the door.

Lenora fell backward away from the armored girl. As she fell, she reached out . . .

. . . and her hand tore at the girl's padded armor, and she grabbed on, and gripped hard . . .

. . . and a piece of armor on the girl's chest tore loose as Lenora fell . . .

. . . and as she fell, she could see what lay beneath the padded armor on the girl's chest . . .

It was a librarian's badge.

And Lenora's eyes widened as she read the words there, and she looked up at the girl, whose expression behind the mask was unknowable . . .

And then Lenora was tumbling down a steep slide, head over heels, her thoughts spinning at the words she had just read, until she fell through a small square portal with a door that instantly slid shut behind her. It slid shut so perfectly that where there had once been a door, you could not now tell there had been anything but a wall.

Lenora was lying on a cool hardwood floor. Cedar beams stretched up to the high ceiling above her.

She was between two bookshelves, just around the corner from the large and heavy archway above which, she knew, the words KNOWLEDGE IS A LIGHT had been deeply chiseled. She leapt to her feet—and felt a hand seize her shoulder.

"There you are!"

And she looked up to see the most terrible thing she had ever seen: the scowling face of the nanny.

"No!" yelled Lenora, and she tried to run, but the nanny had her by the hand and was already dragging her away.

"You naughty girl," said the nanny. "You've cost me ten minutes searching for you! Now I'm going to be late. Your parents *will* be notified."

Lenora dug in her heels and would not budge. She looked desperately for the archway—

But it was no longer there. The nanny tossed Lenora over her shoulder and stalked through the library as astonished patrons looked on.

"No!" shouted Lenora. "I have a job! I work here! I'm Queen of the Penguins!"

But the nanny would not listen, of course, and they marched down toward the exit, Lenora yelling the whole way. As they passed the front desk, Lenora looked pleadingly at the librarian sitting there.

But the librarian put her finger to her lips, shushing Lenora, and Lenora could not help but go quiet. And then—

The librarian smiled and gave Lenora a broad wink—

And then they were out the door and into the sunshine and marching down the steps to where Lenora could see the chauffeur folding up his newspaper as he saw them approach. And she looked back for one last view of the library, its front door swinging shut, and her heart broke to think of all she was leaving behind, the books upon books, all the wisdom of all times past, present, and future, and all the adventures that awaited those who were armed with the light of knowledge, but she knew, she knew, because she had seen the older girl's badge, and on the badge were words that were simple but summed up everything:

LENORA

———— ◦ ⁝ ◦ ————

LIBRARIAN

And she knew, she knew . . .

SHE
WOULD
BE
BACK!

ACKNOWLEDGMENTS

Zeno Alexander would like to thank the following for *The Library of Ever*: the lovely and wise Miriam Angress, the crack team of wordsmiths who style themselves Adverb Fight Club (John Claude Bemis, Jennifer Harrod, and J.J. Johnson), and the relentlessly encouraging Anjali Banerjee. Furthermore, to Claudia Lanese for her artistic inspiration, and Matt Rockefeller for his glorious artwork. Melinda Wang's advice, as always, was invaluable. Also, Paige Wheeler and the team at Creative Media Agency, who kicked down Zeno's door and wrested this manuscript from his hands, then turned it over to John Morgan at Imprint, who, along with Erin Stein, Ellen Duda, Dawn Ryan, Raymond Ernesto Colón, and Bethany Reis, crafted it into the book you are holding now. And of course, the utmost gratitude to Lenora, who allowed Zeno to tell her story.

Zeno may be reached via electronic post at zenoalexander@pm.me

Lenora returns—but finds the Library is not as she left it—in *Rebel in the Library of Ever*.

KEEP READING FOR AN EXCERPT.

CHAPTER ONE
Lenora Returns

Lenora was bruised and battered.

She slumped against the wall of the dojo in her uniform and mask, feeling utterly beaten. Everything ached. Everyone else at the kendo dojo was much older, taller, and stronger than Lenora, not to mention much more experienced in the Japanese martial art of sword-fighting. Battling them was hopeless. And she could tell they were taking it easy on her, too, which only made her get angrier and fight harder.

Even getting into the class had been a struggle.

"I'm sorry," the sensei, a very nice old man, had said when she'd first showed up. "But we don't have enough interested children to start a children's class."

I *don't* want *a children's class*, Lenora almost snarled, then stopped herself. The teacher meant well, after all. "I need to study kendo, sensei," she told him, bowing. "I need to become a master, because—" She hesitated. She couldn't tell him the true reason. He would never believe her, any more than her parents had.

"I got a job at the library!" she'd announced to her parents with excitement after her return from her first adventures at the otherworldly library that spanned all of space and time.

"I told you, Lenora," her father had said. "Libraries don't hire eleven-year-olds."

"But it's true," she said. "And there were space-ships, and I shrank to the size of an ant, and . . ." She stopped. Her parents were staring at her with alarm.

"That's . . . fascinating, dear," her mother said with concern. "You've always had such a vivid imagination. Maybe you should write this all down. We could show it to a nice doctor."

After that, Lenora had learned to keep silent about the Library—for that was how she thought of it now, with a capital *L*, and its name "not written in ink but in a golden splash," to quote one of Lenora's favorite books.

"Because," she had said to the sensei, "I—I— really like kendo. Please let me try." Lenora winced at her weak response. But she could not tell the truth.

The sensei had pondered this, chin in hand, looking Lenora up and down. "I would not normally do this," he said. "But there is something about you . . . I will allow you to try. It will be very difficult, you know."

Lenora was not worried about that. If only the teacher knew how very many difficult things she had already overcome.

Now, a year later, as she leaned against the wall, her entire body begging for mercy, the sensei approached and removed his mask. He smiled at her kindly, and, she could tell with irritation, a bit of pity. "I admire your fighting spirit, Lenora," he said. "But this really isn't the place for a twelve-year-old."

"I must study kendo, sensei," she told him, bowing despite her aches and pains. "I need to become a master, because years in the future, I'm going to have to fight off three robots wielding two swords each in pitch darkness, and I need to be ready."

"I see," said the sensei, putting his mask back on. "Well, back at it, then." He returned to the group of fighters whirling about, shouting and hitting one another with their bamboo swords. Over the past year, the sensei had gotten quite used to the occasional odd phrase slipping through Lenora's lips, and they had developed a silent agreement that he would not ask any further questions.

Lenora thought about returning to the fray. But she had to admit to herself that she had had enough for one night. Her parents had been completely mystified as to why Lenora had demanded to take kendo classes six nights a week, but they had finally agreed. They were also confused as to why she wanted to spend her remaining free hours after

school at the library, reading, but after much argu-
ing and pleading from Lenora they had allowed her
to take the bus by herself so that she could go anytime she wanted.

Lenora had tried to get back to the Library. She
had searched every inch of the regular library with
its lovely, large windows through which sunlight
poured eagerly in, and beautiful cedar beams that
stretched up to the high ceiling. But she hadn't
found a way in. She'd asked the librarians, but
they would only smile mysteriously and change the
subject. So Lenora knew she'd have to be patient,
however much she hated that.

She knew that when she *did* get back, she had
to be ready. Ready not only to help her patrons,
but to fight the Forces of Darkness, who were the
enemies of knowledge and wore black bowler hats
and would try to devour her the first chance they
got. She'd faced them several times before, and the
experiences had been so harrowing that she still
jumped every time a person in a black hat passed
her on the street.

And so Lenora could only read book after book

after book, and get herself whacked around by kendo swords, and wait as a year passed.

One Saturday morning she was lying in her favorite spot at the library, a window seat that was sunny all day long, reading about the Battle of Pelusium and wondering if it really *had* been fought with cats. She'd met a time traveler in the Library who might be able to tell her, and resolved to ask him the next time she saw him.

The library had been oddly quiet all morning. Lenora realized it had been a long time since she'd seen any patrons, or any librarians. Closing her book, she got up to investigate. She went out into the wide-open atrium at the center of the library and looked in all directions. She didn't see anyone, not even any librarians behind the reference desk.

Then a librarian swerved into view, walking swiftly from the back of the building. As the woman got closer, Lenora saw she was crying and carrying a cardboard box. Lenora ran to her. Her name was Aaliyah, and she was one of Lenora's favorites. "What's wrong?" Lenora asked, alarmed.

Aaliyah stopped, sniffling. "I've been fired," she said through her tears.

"What?" said Lenora, outraged. "Whyever would they fire you?" For Aaliyah, in Lenora's expert opinion, was one of the best.

Aaliyah looked in all directions. It was as though she suspected someone was watching or listening to them. Then she beckoned Lenora off to the side, into a narrow space between two stacks. She looked around again, then knelt and whispered into Lenora's ear: "The Library needs you. You have to hurry!" And from the way she said it, Lenora knew exactly which Library she meant.

Then Aaliyah stood, took one more fearful look around, and moved to leave.

"Wait!" said Lenora in a loud whisper. "Don't leave. Stay and fight! I'll find a way to save your job, I promise."

Lenora knew that if she had said such a thing to any other adult, they would have simply patted her on her head and called her adorable.

But not Aaliyah. Aaliyah was a librarian. And she knew.

The woman put her box on the floor. "Very well," she said in a whisper. "I will try. But I don't know how long I can manage. Please hurry, Lenora!"

And then she strode quickly away, toward one of the deepest corners of this library.

Lenora stood there, stunned. *The Library needs you.* But why? And what could she do to help? She had no idea even how to get back to it.

While she stood there, she noticed a woman and a boy approach the reference desk and look around curiously, doubtless wondering why there wasn't a librarian in sight.

There was nothing else for Lenora to do. She strode over to the desk and went behind it, her heart pounding with excitement at being back behind a reference desk.

"Hello," said Lenora. "How may I help you?"

The lady peered down her nose at Lenora. "Aren't you a little young to work here?"

"Try me," replied Lenora.

"Well," said the woman, hesitating.

The boy spoke up. "I need to know what the world's largest number is."

"I already told him the largest number is infinity," said the woman. "But he won't listen."

"Infinity isn't really a number," said Lenora. She'd gotten deeply into the math section that fall.

"Of course it is," said the woman. "Everyone knows that. I want to speak to a real librarian."

Lenora drew herself up to her full height, which admittedly wasn't much. She wished she were ten feet tall like Chief Answerer Malachi, the imposing woman who had given Lenora her job at the Library along with several most interesting assignments. Malachi could have looked down her nose at this woman instead of peering up at her from below, as Lenora was forced to do. "I *am* a real librarian, and infinity is *not* the world's largest number."

"If you're a real librarian," challenged the woman, "then where is your badge?"

Lenora was crushed. Her badge, which listed many of her greatest accomplishments at the Library, had vanished upon her departure a year ago. She still had her library card, which she wore on a string around her neck next to her heart, where it glowed faintly and even hummed from time to time (she had no idea why), but the badge was gone.

"I left it in the staff room," lied Lenora. "I'll get it and I'll get the answer to your question." Maybe another librarian had left a badge lying around and Lenora could use that. She didn't feel this was a deception. She really *was* a librarian, and an excellent one at that. Also, she didn't like the woman and wanted to help the boy get the right answer.

The staff room was right behind the reference desk. She marched in. The room had comfortable-looking tables and chairs and a counter with a sink and small microwave oven. There were some desks, too, but no badges to be seen. She went farther in. In the back there were some shelves, rather messily organized, with stacks of papers and journals and books and supplies. She dashed through the shelves, looking everywhere for a badge. But there was none to be found. The woman would never believe her, and the boy would not get the right answer. There was no worse feeling for Lenora.

Somehow she seemed to have gotten turned

around. There had only been a few shelves, but no matter which way she turned, she kept coming back to them. She couldn't find the area with the tables and sink and microwave.

She was lost. A thrill ran through her. This had happened before, and . . . was it possible?

Lenora realized her library card was humming. She pulled it out from beneath her shirt. It was blazing with glorious light, the words LIBRARY CARD glittering with all the colors of the rainbow, and it was fluttering about like a butterfly. Lenora grasped hold of it tightly.

She remembered the words of her much older, future self, Lenora the kendo master, who had given Lenora the library card and said: *When the time comes, you will need this. Don't worry, you'll know.*

Lenora needed this. Hoping against hope, she did the only thing she could think of. She gripped the card, closed her eyes, and whispered the phrase whose meaning she had learned when clutched in the very grip of the Forces, within their cold, impenetrable dark:

"Knowledge Is a Light."

There was a tremendous crack, like a granite boulder splitting open. Lenora opened her eyes, and there, to her great delight, was a massive stone archway in the wall where none had been before, above which a phrase had been deeply chiseled:

KNOWLEDGE IS A LIGHT

Shrieking with joy, Lenora raced through the archway and into the tunnel beyond. Though as she did, she noticed something was different. She had seen these words before, so sharply chiseled, but now they looked weathered and worn, as though no one had been maintaining them for ages. But it didn't matter, she was back in the Library, and she couldn't be more excited.

Her excitement ended when she reached the end of the tunnel.

CHAPTER TWO
Lenora Learns

Lenora looked forward to seeing the Library again, with its vast and dazzling towers, endless stacks of books, giant windows with infinite vistas beyond, and blimps and tubes and talking whales and whatever other marvels the Library might toss her way.

But this did not happen.

The tunnel ended in the most depressing, low-ceilinged room, cramped with completely empty bookshelves shoved together haphazardly, with horrid neon bulbs flickering dismally above. The floor was dirty tile and all the whitish walls were bare.

Lenora took a deep breath, steadying herself. This was nothing like the dreams she'd been having of her magnificent return to the Library. She had all the information she needed to know that something was Terribly Wrong.

Then she felt a fluttering on her chest, right in front of her heart. She looked down to see that a badge had appeared there, and the badge said

LENORA

———◦╎◦———

SECOND APPRENTICE LIBRARIAN

This was unimaginably reassuring. Despite things being Terribly Wrong, she had her badge back, she was still a librarian, and she had a job to do. And judging from her new title, she'd even gotten a promotion from Third Apprentice, her final title when she had last been in the Library. She hoped that meant she wouldn't be fired somehow, like Aaliyah had been. Steeling herself for whatever was to come, she looked around for an exit—for she knew the first thing she had to do was locate Chief Answerer Malachi and find out what was going on.

She wandered through the shelves, noting that none of them were the least bit dusty, and so must have been emptied recently. At last she came to a door, which she pushed open to find a long hallway lined with more doors, and more dirty tile and flickering lights. It all looked like a scene from those television shows about adults who hate their jobs, and Lenora was beginning to wonder if she was actually in the Library at all.

She was disappointed to see no sign of a Tube station, the tubes being the main means of travel through the vast Library, whooshing librarians along in glass tubes that could take them almost anywhere. But then she remembered she no longer had a Tube key, and so she could not use the system even if she wanted to.

There was nowhere to go but forward, so forward she went.

As she passed, she could see all the doors were open, and beyond each was a small office with nothing in it but a beat-up desk and chair. After about ten or twelve of these, Lenora jumped a little when she passed one with a woman sitting in it. The woman was sitting at the desk with hands folded, staring at the wall. She was wearing a red raincoat on which was a badge that said LIBRARIAN with no name. She turned her head slowly to look at Lenora. Something behind her eyes flickered. And beneath that raincoat, a snake-like something slithered over her shoulder.

Goose bumps rose on Lenora's arms, and she knew. The Forces of Darkness. The flickering and slithering told her, but somehow, she knew that she would have recognized this creature for what it was even without those things. Perhaps she would think about that later, because the woman had already stood and was stalking toward her.

Lenora was a girl of action. She had learned to venture forth boldly and rely on her wits and valor. But somehow, she could not move. Her feet felt bolted to the floor. Sweat broke out all over her and she began to shake. In the most dangerous moments, Lenora had always kept her head. But now she was simply terrified. She felt, rising within her, a scream.

The woman came close and leaned over, studying Lenora's eyes. "Who are you?" she asked in a voice that sent more waves of terror through Lenora. *Run!* her mind begged. But she could not.

"I—I'm a librarian," Lenora squeaked, humiliated at the sound of her own voice.

"How nice," the woman said. Something wriggled beneath her coat. "But I have not seen you before. Perhaps you do not know that librarians are not so welcome here these days. You may choose to quit, be fired, or cooperate. If you do none of those things, we will, of course, eat you. Choose. Now."

Lenora had heard such a threat before. *I say we eat her now and get it over with,* a monster like this woman had once said about Lenora. She closed her eyes, remembering that moment, and what Malachi had told her afterward: *Knowledge Is a Light, Lenora.* Everything Malachi had said at the time was forever etched in Lenora's mind, as though chiseled in stone: *Throughout history, that light has at times burned very dimly, and nearly even gone out, while in other times it has blazed up gloriously.*

As she remembered those words, she was surprised to hear a sudden hiss. She opened her eyes, and was shocked to see the woman flinching back, away from Lenora. For the briefest moment, she looked down at her hands. Was she glowing, as she had glowed once before? There seemed to be something, barely visible under the harsh light . . . but there was no time to think about it. All her fear had vanished, and she could move again. But already the woman in the raincoat was recovering.

Lenora wasted no time in breaking into a full run. In her career the Forces had made any number of attempts to squish or eat or attack her with swords, and she wasn't about to wait around to find out what this one, who was more terrifying than all the rest put together, would do.